D0148133

Richmond Macabre

Nightmares From the River City

Edited By
Beth Brown and Phil Ford

Cover Art By
Noah Scalin

This is a work of fiction. Names, characters, places, and incidents are either products of the authors' imaginations or, if real, are used fictitiously.

Introduction copyright © 2011 by Harry Kollatz, Jr.
"Vampire Fiction" copyright © 2011 by Charles Albert
"The Rememberist" copyright © 2011 by Michael Gray Baughan
"Mr. Valdemar" copyright © 2011 by Beth Brown
"The Third Office" copyright © 2011 by Dale Brumfield
"Sig's Place" copyright © 2011 by Phil Budahn
"Hunting Joey Banks" copyright © 2011 by Meriah L. Crawford
"The Velveteen Machine" copyright © 2011 by James Ebersole
"231 Creeper" copyright © 2011 by Phil D. Ford
"Gamble's Hill" copyright © 2011 by Daniel Gibbs
"The Conjurer" copyright © 2011 by Andrew Goethals
"The Bike Chain of Fate" copyright © 2011 by Eric Hill
"Everything Must Go" copyright © 2011 by Melissa Scott Sinclair
"We're History" copyright © 2011 by Rebecca Snow
"Dirt and Iron" copyright © 2011 by Dawn Terrizzi
"Maggie" copyright © 2011 by Amber Timmerman

All rights reserved. No part of this book may be reproduced, transmitted, or stored in an information retrieval system in any form or by any means, graphic, electronic, or mechanical, including photocopying, taping, and recording, without prior written permission from the publisher.

First paperback edition 2011

Library of Congress Cataloging In Publication Data

Richmond Macabre: Nightmares From the River City /
Edited by Beth Brown and Phil Ford. – 1st ed.
p. cm.
Contents: Vampire Fiction / Charles Albert – The Rememberist / Michael Gray Baughan – Mr. Valdemar / Beth Brown – The Third Office – Dale Brumfield – Sig's Place / Phil Budahn – Hunting Joey Banks / Meriah L. Crawford – The Velveteen Machine / James Ebersole – 231 Creeper / Phil D. Ford – Gamble's Hill / Daniel Gibbs – The Conjurer / Andrew Goethals – The Bike Chain of Fate / Eric Hill – Everything Must Go / Melissa Scott Sinclair – We're History / Rebecca Snow – Dirt and Iron / Dawn Terrizzi – Maggie / Amber Timmerman.

ISBN 978-0-9838914-0-6

2 4 6 8 10 9 7 5 3 1

Printed in the United States of America.

Iron Cauldron Books
Richmond, Virginia
www.IronCauldronBooks.com

For Edgar

Contents

Introduction:
Being a True Relation

Harry Kollatz, Jr.

"[Edgar Allan Poe] disliked the dark and rarely went out when I knew him. On one occasion he said to me, 'I believe that demons take advantage of the night to mislead the unwary--although you know,' he added, 'I don't believe in them.' --Philadelphia publisher George R. Graham

In a misty far-off age before Ubiquitous Internet and sometime in the Second Reagan Administration I conjured a business that I figured couldn't miss. In Richmond, where history is a growth industry, and in neighborhoods where the plucky and foolhardy were becoming the latest stewards of creaky old houses, seemed to me people wanted to know their place in the current of events. I came up with Who Slept Here? Services to research and create house histories. My first territory would be the Fan District.

I divided the reports by costs of packages. The cheapest was the gleaning from a mere city directory search that generated a list of past residents and their occupations. The second upgrade also included how the client's street got its name and a brief history of the Fan.

"The Cellar To The Dome" edition featured a narrative history of the house derived from tracking down past residents and asking

about their lives there in addition to a chain-of-title search --
something lawyers charged a huge amount of money to
accomplish. Further included were printed photographs of a
historic variety and an illustration of the house. Maybe I charged
$300 for the whole thing. I even hired a typist because my
accuracy in those days, and my impatience with white out, wasn't
up to professional standard.

These reports were time consuming thus I didn't complete
many of them. Since one tended to fund the next they didn't earn
much money, either.

During conversations for almost all of the histories I either
researched or was contacted about, there was a question like:
"Maybe you can explain why we hear a child crying in the back
room when we don't have children." Or, "Do you think you can tell
us why there's this orb of light that shows up at the top of the
stairs and moves down the hall?"

Seriously.

I explained, somewhat huffily: I'm an historian. Not a ghost
buster.

Years later, when writing for the city magazine, I'd
periodically need to track down one ghost story or another.
Richmond, when you looked at the lore, and by that I mean the
oeuvre of L.B. Taylor and Marguerite Du Pont Lee, the city is
somewhat a dry patch for publicly known ghost stories. (Emphasis
on *publicly* known) And oftentimes, the legend persisted although
the house didn't exist anymore, like the lady with the tortoise shell
comb, who allegedly unnerved residents of the Hawes House at
506 E. Leigh St. That elegant 1816 residence was demolished in
1968, victim of the "bomb the village to save it" mentality of the

City Center "renewal" crowd. Talk about Richmond macabre.

What's important for us is not whether Richmond is actually pound-for-pound more haunted than say, Charleston, Savannah or New Orleans – sisters in our sorority. What's germane is Richmond's Eldritch Quotient. EQ measures the potential for the weird and eerie in a specific locality. The EQ isn't as much a numeric rating but a layering of impressions.

Look at Richmond: In Hollywood Cemetery alone there are approximately 18,000 Confederate soldiers, a spooky pyramid and the reputed vampire W.W. Poole (whose initials, after all, resemble fangs). Then there are the battlefields and the numerous warehouses used as prisons and hospitals.

Interwoven and inextricable to all of that are the 400 years of slavery and before that, the 10,000 years of native people living along this undulant curve of Mother James.

We've had our share of curious characters and odd events, strange murders and historic duels over editorials and love. All this sets a tone -- and this is important, when writing a tale set here. Richmond is an old town. Cobbled alleyways wend between narrow streets where in some neighborhoods houses are pushing two centuries. Big grey stone buildings hove from out of heavy autumn fogs seeming the perfect places of capture for the un-flown and the undead. Once, there was even a psychic horse. But that's another story.

The accumulation of all these impressions and expressions gives Richmond an impressive EQ.

A personal house history experience lends some credence, leastwise to me, that there's something going on here and we don't know quite what it is.

A long time ago, around about 1982, I lived in an old Queen Anne townhouse in the 1600 block of Grove Avenue. I'd learn that it was converted into a rooming house in the middle of the Depression, as was the fate of many of the larger Richmond city houses. During those days I worked as a copy clerk at the Richmond Times-Dispatch. I made coffee and shot page proofs to the composing room through a pneumatic tube. Text and ads were set into dummy pages by wax before they were photographed. It was almost steampunk.

Down in the morgue where rows of file cabinets kept the collective subconscious of thousands of issues of the city's newspapers in the form of clip files and photo folders. There was also a huge set of the Richmond city directories that went back near as I recall to the 1890s.

Guy like me wanted to go down there and never come out. It made researching the house where I then lived incredibly easy. I learned that its first owner was Olive Branch Morgan, so-named for the boat he was born on to his Welsh immigrant parents, and he and his numerous children lived there while he was an executive for the Virginia-Carolina Chemical Co. – a fertilizer firm. Then came Dr. Frederick Kellam and his sons who ran the Kellam Cancer Hospital (more of this anon). Then there was Robert and Maude Hudson. Robert was an inventor of improved railroad crossing gates and an anti-aircraft machine gun that interested the military in the 1930s. Maude was involved in the women's rights movement. Through their acquaintance came sister suffragist and activist Dr. Helen Love Bossieux. She also at certain times claimed as her profession numerologist, astrologer and on occasion, "poetess." The newspapers consulted Helen for New Year's predictions and other occasional insights. Her biography was repeated without question, including being a graduate of the Columbia School of Physicians and Surgeons. Turns out she grafted onto her own *vitae* the career of her actual first husband, Dr. Lee Bailey Pultz from upstate New York.

She was involved in a protracted divorce against Husband #2, Carlton Lee Bossieux, who'd apparently tried to fake his death in the big 1927 Florida hurricane, but then exhibited the characteristic poor sense to return home to Mother. Helen, riding a trolley on a hot summer afternoon and seated next to an open window, heard a familiar smoker's cough. She gazed down and sure enough, there was Lee. She jotted down the license plate of his "machine" as the paper described it. Sooner than you can say, "You've been served" her un-divorced scofflaw spouse got slapped for desertion. And that was just the beginning.

All this material came out of one house, a rather commonplace Queen Anne resembling many others of its antique vintage throughout Fan. Turned out that my housemates and I were but one in a long succession of eccentrics.

And then there was the noise.

Every other night, around 3 a.m., I was startled awake by a clumping, dragging disturbance from the floor above. The noise rumbled diagonally from one far corner to the other. One time, the vibration was strong enough to rattle change on the nightstand. I asked the house manager, a perennial political candidate and former minister Roger Coffey, if he'd ever heard anything out of the ordinary. "Ah, yeah," he uncertainly muttered. "People say they've heard stuff, you know, it's an old house. I feel a little weird here myself sometimes."

No one lived above me, or in the front part of the parlor separated by the sliding door that was the jackleg bedroom's wall. The house next door stood vacant. During one holiday or another, when nobody else was in the house, I somehow inveigled friends to position them throughout it at the appointed hour. And I was proved not to be hearing things. One of my friends said, "It sounds almost like the house is groaning."

Remember the Kellams? My research on them revealed that for thirty years the family operated a clinic where they claimed to cure cancer. Their ads exhorted that any mole or wart on the skin was cancerous needing immediate removal. They told visitors to come see the cancers they'd removed ("They are wonderful!") that the Kellams had somehow displayed as evidence of the efficacy of their procedures. An old physician who'd known of their questionable practices informed me that the Kellams probably used a zinc-based paste to eat skin. The resulting disfigurement was beyond the day's corrective surgery. Some patients went to the hospital as a last hope. The Kellams offered to pay the train fare of some these unfortunates who benefited neither from the doctors' largesse nor their medical knowledge. Fred Kellam, the paterfamilias, died of a heart attack in the upstairs bedroom I later occupied.

If this doesn't amp up the EQ factor, I don't know what would.

For many years the Kellam Cancer Hospital's location was the 1600 block of West Main. The dignified three-story brick building was demolished in the 1940s for a soda pop warehouse that in 2011 is occupied by the Try-Me gallery space. When I found an image of the Kellam Hospital at the Valentine Museum it was really as though I'd seen a ghost. Which is what pictures are: light of a moment captured and sent forward in time.

But none of this quite explained the grumbling in the ceiling.

At the time, some friends of mine fancied themselves as mystics or whatnot. They wore crystals, read about Aleister Crowley and played around with tarot cards. There was a considerable amount of consciousness altering though, I daresay, little consciousness-raising. The head mysterion of this little band fancied himself as a communicator to other worlds. He used a DIY Ouija board that used for a platen an overturned glass ashtray with felt glued to its corners for movement across a glass top.

One night he brought over some of his adherents and a few girls and sought to contact the spirits making the ruckus. Much excitement followed. The ashtray heated up. The board spat out curse words, the Demonic number, made reference to Kellams and murder and cackled at one of the girls as a virgin. And she was. They practically ran out of the room.

But don't you know, from that night on, I never lost a moment of sleep due to noises from that ceiling — at least, not of a spectral nature, but more carnal.

You will find in this collection a definite acknowledgment of Richmond's EQ in all its variations. For example, Melissa Scott Sinclair's "Everything Must Go" puts a ripped-from-recent-headlines spin on a twice-told tale that is both humorous and moving. In "Maggie," Amber Timmerman takes obsessive-compulsive to an entirely new level and makes every bad first date you've had look good by comparison. "Vampire Fiction" by Charles Albert takes on the current cultural fascination without glamour, but a sudden twist. Michael Gray Baughan persuasively returns us to Civil War-era Richmond in his story that redefines self-actualization.

These stories put Richmond's EQ off the charts.

Vampire Fiction

Charles Albert

"Then Roderick sweeps Esmeralda up in his arms and bares his fangs. He bites her and she is turned into a vampire. The two turn into smoke and drift up onto the rooftops where they make love," Jane explained matter-of-factly. There was a tinge of wistfulness to her voice that made one wonder if she realized it was just a TV show. "That's where last season ended."

Dominique, a shorter, rounder woman than Jane, eyed her up and down. She worried about her friend's obsession with all of these vampire stories. Ever since it became trendy, Jane had little by little changed. First it was harmless, like getting her hair cut like the actress on TV. Then it was the black clothing (cut way too tight for a woman in her mid-thirties, Dominique thought.) But then, Jane started getting vampire tattoos and going to the fan conventions. Every lunch break she would re-read the same worn-out copy of the book that started her whole obsession. And the body glitter!

"I know you are excited for the new season of your show, but just Tivo it or something and come out to the club with me. We'll have a drink and maybe meet some guys." Dominique tried appealing to her friend but doubted it would work.

While the possibility of meeting some men would have once been enticing to her, Jane's loneliness had ceased long ago when she started reading her "stories," as she called them. She had never known acceptance, but she didn't worry about fitting in anymore. She was outside of the "normal" world, much like the vampires in her stories. Without a moment's hesitation she replied, "I have been waiting months for the new season to start. I am not missing it."

"You might just," croaked a raspy voice from behind the two women. Startled, they turned around to find Gary, a short, bald toad of a man with much too pale skin and a hideous fashion sense – a short-sleeved Oxford shirt with a mauve tie. What was he thinking? He was in Jane's and Dominique's group, angling for a supervisor position that he would never get. How he had glided up behind her so silently was beyond Jane, but she knew that whenever he spoke to her, it only ever caused her headaches.

"Can we help you Gary?" Dominique said through gritted teeth with just a little bit of sass.

"Mr. Henderson needs a list of all journal entries you made this quarter and how they impacted the balance sheet." One could smell the stale coffee breath wafting through the air as he talked.

"I am about to go on lunch," explained Jane as she held her vampire romance novel in front of her as if to say, "I have more important things to do."

"I don't know why you waste your time with those vampire stories. You know vampires aren't real." Gary blinked hard.

"I know," Jane lied. "It's just a form of escape."

"Hmph," Gary sighed. "So long as it gets done tonight. I told Mr. Henderson it would be on his desk first thing tomorrow morning." Abruptly Gary turned and left the break room. Jane noticed the way he moved. It was entirely effortless. She wondered how that was possible for someone of Gary's girth, but the thought left her head half-coalesced as she did not deign to worry about it anymore.

Dominique explained that she did not want to stay late working on Gary's request, removed her lunch from the microwave where they had been standing, and – after the two women exchanged pleasantries – proceeded back to her desk. Jane stood there alone holding her book in one hand and her brown lunch bag in the other. She contemplated returning to her desk and eating while working on the arduous and arbitrary request of her boss, but she knew that she was only ten or so pages away from Remy revealing to Esmeralda that he was in fact an ancient, Egyptian mummy. Ten pages, then she would return to finish the task at hand and still make it home in time for her TV show. Her feet began walking to the elevator before she had even finished her thought.

Jane liked to eat lunch outside, down by the canal. It was a short walk from her office building in the heart of Richmond's busy commercial center down to the sunny spot where she liked to read and unwind. It was nice to have a mental break in the middle of the day, to get away from the dreary horrors of office life. She had gone to college in Richmond wanting to be an artist. When her degree was earned, however, she found it very difficult to use. She found herself taking office jobs, at first just to make ends meet while her art career picked up. It had been months since she had even touched a paintbrush however. While not physically or mentally taxing, her current job drained her spiritually. Crunching away on numbers representing hypothetical sums of other people's money too large to even seem real, all the while putting up with trolls like Gary. After forty hours a week of that, she found it impossible to be moved enough to paint.

Jane thought about all of this as she absent-mindedly fumbled through her book, sitting in front of the canal, smelling the fresh air and hearing the gentle lapping of the water against its artificial banks. She had only intended to read ten pages, but while retreading familiar literary ground and deep in thought, she worked her way through the rest of the entire book. It was only when she reached the back cover with its smiling photograph of the author staring at her lovingly that she realized she had sat there for too long. Looking around, she noticed that half the afternoon was wasted and that if she wanted to see her precious TV show, she would need to hurry to finish her work back at the office.

The rest of the afternoon was a blur. People dropped off memos at Jane's desk, but she never looked up from her computer screen to acknowledge their comings or goings. She feverishly banged away at her keyboard, the whole time cursing herself for taking such a long lunch. If she missed her show, she would have to wait a whole week for them to upload it to the internet! Then she would be off by a week the entire season while she waited for the new episodes to go up. Such indignity.

Dominique stopped by at a quarter after five. She said something to Jane about blowing off the assignment and coming to the club with her. Jane waved her off and refocused her efforts on the task at hand. It had not occurred to her to just blow the assignment off. She supposed that she could get away with it – make up some sob story about having to go home early. Who was she kidding though? Mr. Henderson had a family, and he still worked ridiculously long hours. Who was Jane going home to, her cats? Thoughts began to swirl. If she stayed and finished, she could still conceivably make it home in time. If she left now, however, she could end up jobless and on the street. In this economy, while as far-fetched as blowing off one assignment and being fired might seem, Jane feared the outcome all the same.

As the hours ticked by, her regret and frustration turned from an ashamed, self-hatred to an outward manifestation toward the one whose fault this really was – at least as Jane saw it – Gary. If he had not promised the report to Mr. Henderson by first-thing next morning, she would not be in this situation.

Jane hated Gary, and not just for her current predicament. He had always been so strange and such a jerk. While it was not uncommon for people to bring leftovers for lunch, Gary brought a big, bloody raw steak for lunch every day. The sight and smell of that sitting in the fridge first thing in the morning often made Jane's stomach crawl.

Thinking of his lunch made Jane recall an incident where she watched him throw her lunch away. When she called him out on it, he had the nerve to say, "Well, you should have put your name on it." He knew that it had been her lunch, Jane was convinced, but threw it away out of spite.

Then there was six months ago when he petitioned the office manager to start buying special, UV-minimal lighting for the area around their cubicals. Gary complained that he had a skin allergy and was very sensitive to UV light, but the result meant a harsher light which often gave Jane headaches.

Gary could never leave well enough alone. He was always looking for "process improvements," corporate buzzwords which mean "do things the hard way." If he ever did get promoted to the supervisor position, Jane would have to quit. It was bad enough to deal with the man as an equal, but the thought of giving that man any kind of power was absolutely sickening.

Mentally griping about Gary did not slow Jane at her work. Without even double-checking the spreadsheet, upon completion, Jane saved it as an attachment and sent it to Mr. Henderson. In one, swift move, she stood-up, grabbed her purse and shut off the computer monitor all at once. She had forty-five minutes until her show premiered and it would be a thirty minute bus ride. Assuming she made the bus with minimal wait time, she wouldn't miss a thing. As she sprinted to the elevator, she noted that Gary's computer monitor was still on, though she hadn't recalled seeing him since everyone else left. No matter.

Finding her way off the elevator and into the street, Jane's heart sank. She had suddenly remembered what had escaped her only moments before. The usual, convenient bus stop directly in front of her building was temporarily moved due to road work. She had to walk several blocks to catch the right bus. In the dark. Alone.

Though it should have, the danger of this journey was not what worried Jane, but rather the time it would take to reach the next bus stop. Resolute, she reached into her purse to find the small can of Mace her uncle had given her when she moved to the city. With it securely in hand, she continued onward.

Her feet pounded the city sidewalk with purpose as she strode along. Street lights kept the trek from being too dismal, but this section of town was all office buildings. It seemed deserted at this time of night. Jane began to muse that she was the lone survivor of some terrible plague, wandering the streets trying to find someone, anyone. This thought sent a chill down her spine, so she dismissed it for another fantasy. She now thought she was a creature of the night, a vampire, hunting and stalking her prey through the man-made canyons of downtown Richmond. This thought filled her with confidence.

So much so, that it did not occur to her to use her mace immediately when someone called out of the pitch-black alley, "Hey!"

She stopped, wheeled around to peer into the inky alleyway. She made out the figure of a man in sweatpants and a large, dirty parka, despite the heat of the night. He was a homeless man. Jane had always felt bad for these denizens of the streets, ever since she first came to school in the city. Growing up in the rural town of Berryville, she did not think such people existed, or at least not anywhere that polite society cohabited. Instinctively she started fishing in her purse for some cash, allowing the Mace can to drop harmlessly to the bottom of her bag.

"You got twenty bucks?" the man responded, seeing Jane going into her purse. If his original intent in stopping her had been sinister, his plan had now changed. Seeing the generosity of Jane, he had decided to see how much he could get without a hassle.

"Sorry, I don't usually carry much cash, but here's two dollars."

The homeless man reached for the crumpled bills roughly. He took them without so much as a "thank-you" and turned and walked down the darkened alley. Jane did not even notice the lack of gratitude as she turned to travel the last two blocks to the bus stop.

Jane didn't even take three steps away from the entry to the dark portal when she froze. The adrenaline of her daydream had worn off and she realized just how much danger she could have been in. Hadn't there been something in the news recently about a homeless guy murdering people? No, that wasn't quite right. Maybe the other way around? Jane could not remember.

She pulled open her purse and frantically began searching for her Mace. It was then that a loud, long, wet scream emanated from the alley way. Jane probably should have run, but instead put her effort into securing the Mace quickly. She found it and clutched it to her chest, but was still frozen in terror. The screaming continued and was so guttural. It did not sound like that on TV.

Jane's fantasy of being a vampire had evaporated like an oil slick in a hot parking lot. Now she could not help but recall the fantasy of being the lone survivor in a desolated city; the only other people, bandits and cannibals. Ironically, Jane did not like the, albeit small, horror elements in her vampire stories. She had always frightened easily.

As suddenly as the screaming started, a hush fell on the alleyway. The trance now broken, Jane began to tell her body to move; fast and in the opposite direction. Before her legs could comply, the homeless man she had just met came running headlong from the darkness covered in blood and clutching his neck. It was not immediately evident if it was his blood or that of a presumed victim. He fell at Jane's feet, looking up at her with desperation in his eyes. Jane, too terrified to read the injured man's body language, turned her can of Mace on the man and proceeded to blind him with the chemical spray.

The man hardly noticed this further slight as he revealed a large, gaping hole where his throat once was. He slumped over on the sidewalk making a gurgling noise reminiscent of the splash of the water against the sides of the canal. Confused and terrified, Jane just stood there, mouth agape, wondering if her self-defensive attack had caused the sanguine damage. Then, with impossible speed and swiftness, a dark object sped from the alley, swooped the man up in its arms in a single, deft move, and returned noiselessly into the dark.

Not trusting her own senses, Jane again peered into the darkness of the alleyway. For a reason that did not make sense even to her, she called out, "Hello?"

There was a rustle in the darkness like dry bones rubbing together. A dark shape hunched over the homeless man's flaccid body. Jane's eyes focused in the dark so that she could better understand what she was seeing. It was Gary! He was covered in blood and fiercely sucking on the homeless man's throat, biting and tearing so that he could reach the sweet, warm juice inside.

"Gary?" Jane was confused.

"Jane," he replied in his usual blunt manner.

"What is going on? Is that guy alright?" There was genuine concern in Jane's voice. This confused Gary.

"He was going to attack you. He had grabbed a weapon and was going to jump you."

Jane was beginning to piece things together. The gore,

dripping from Gary's mouth, while it was grisly, was a tell-tale sign. The low-UV light bulbs in the office and the way he always moved so quietly. Gary was a vampire, and just like Roderick in her stories, he had fallen in love with a mortal woman. He had fallen in love with her!

"You saved me!" she exclaimed as her new-found knowledge spread across her face in a big grin. This was it. This was the chance to have everything she ever wanted. No more menial job, no more loneliness. She crossed to her dark knight and embraced him and blurted, "You are a vampire, aren't you?"

Shorter than her, he thought the embrace was awkward, but knew that his dreams were coming true as well. "Jane," he said, "you have figured it out. It is my... curse. But with you, I know that it can be... uh, a blessing." He struggled to find the words she would want to hear from her stories, and though he only knew of their popularity and not their content, pieced together his speech very deliberately.

"Oh Gary, certainly. Just, tell me..."

"Yes. I will explain all... My, uh, sweet," he forced his words to flourish. Then breaking away from her in a mock-dramatic embellishment, hand on his forehead as he once saw them do in a play, he began to explain: "I have lived for hundreds of years. I was once a European nobleman when I foolishly made a deal with the Devil. Since then, it has been my curse to walk the Earth alone. Have you known loneliness?"

Jane trembled. It was just as she thought. She heaved a breathy sigh, "Yes."

"But now, you and I can be together forever in the twilight

between living and death." He really began to ham it up, seeing that she was buying every word.

"But Gary...?"

"Yes, my dearest?"

"Not to be indelicate, but I always thought that vampires were a bit more... A bit less..." She struggled to find a way to put it. Gary didn't exactly have the physique of the vampires she read about.

Whether seeing her meaning, or just really enjoying his false charisma, Gary swept her back into his arms and whispered, "Vampires can be anything we want to be."

Jane swooned and bared her neck to Gary. This was it, she thought. "Do it."

Gary bit not into the side of her neck, but directly into the jugular. It was not the ginger pricking of the skin by sharp yet gentle fangs like on TV, but rather a hard bite that one would use to break the skin of an apple. With the second bite, Gary ripped at Jane's trachea. Jane tried to scream from the pain, but the shock set in too quickly. The next thing she knew, she saw a dark, wet spray of arterial blood jet from her own neck and against the wall of the alley. Gary continued to gnaw and chew at her soft flesh. Jane found it hard to breathe as her lungs were filling up with fluid. Her last conscious thought was that of her new self when she awoke as a member of the living dead. Would she stay a brunette, or maybe she would try red-head?

The next morning Gary came in fifteen minutes late to the office. Not a standard practice for him, yet with his close relationship to Mr. Henderson, he knew he would not be begrudged an extra fifteen minutes every now and then.

As per his usual morning ritual, he immediately made his way to the break room to deposit his lunch in the fridge. He froze perplexed to find Dominique bawling and hugging Jeff from Human Resources. She noticed Gary standing there sheepishly and ran up to him crying.

"Gary, I have terrible news! Jane was attacked in an alley last night," she sobbed. Gary better understood the emotion than the words themselves as they fell garbled out of her mouth.

"Oh. ... Oh, is she okay?" He bluffed.

"She's dead!" Dominique wailed. "I should have made her leave early." Jeff came up to her and put his arm around her shoulder in a move that should have sent him to one of his own sexual harassment seminars.

Jeff explained the situation as he tried to maneuver Dominique out of the break room, "That serial killer that has been in the news? The one that has been attacking homeless guys? They think Jane interrupted one of his attacks, so he killed her too." Then his voice got real low, "They say he's a cannibal."

The killer was all over the news. Some were comparing him to Jack the Ripper. Other reports included the fact that the murderer had left bite marks on his victims and was known to carve large portions of flesh from them. Jane should have known all this.

At this point, Dominique had become a quivering mess, so Jeff steered her out of the break room. Alone, Gary was able to smile as he continued his normal morning ritual. Opening the fridge, he removed from his shoulder bag a large, clear Tupperware container clearly marked with his name. Inside was an eight-ounce chunk of bloodied meat. Gary stopped as a morbid notion occurred to him. He laughed to himself for a second and wondered if maybe he should have put Jane's name on it instead. It would have only been fitting.

The Rememberist

Michael Gray Baughan

When I was a boy my mother warned me away from my wicked interests, lest they overcome my better nature, but alas I did not heed her. As a man I have learned to keep them on a short tether and only let out the slack when the occasion warrants. Verily has my vocation been a blessing for that. Forty-two years of calamity reportage have allowed me to feed and shelter my unhealthy fixations behind the caul of journalism, but they have also taught me that the unwashed masses share a large measure of my predilection. Enough at least to double sales of the *Dispatch* whenever one of my more grisly columns darkened the page. And though shortages in certain items became commonplace in Richmond as those infernal Yanks marched their agenda ever closer, we never lacked in news of the terrible. Of that we had a-plenty, particularly in the summer of '63, when I finally slaked my thirst for the unspeakable and discovered that there are things even I cannot abide.

I was living on Fourth Street at the time, in a small flat above an unscrupulous apothecary. This afforded me ample opportunity both to witness and be victimized by all manner of common crime. With no less than three brothels, five pubs, and two gambling houses within a short stroll, easy marks with coin-leaden pockets were plentiful around Shockoe after sunfall. Misdemeanors did not interest me much, though. I sought the mark of Cain, as I was known to exclaim too often and too loudly to anyone within earshot after a pint too many of Alsop's Most Excellent Ale. And by that I meant gruesome turns of fate and violent acts of passion. Like the octoroon house girl who just last month poisoned fourteen Shifletts over in Cumberland, only to fall victim to a water moccasin while making her escape. Or when Second Lieutenant Scott of the Virginia Cavalry entertained his men one night during the Battle of Chancellorsville by donning the garb of a dead Yankee and dancing through camp, only to have his Negro boy run him through with his own sword.

Duels were also excellent fodder, with their requisite back stories and often mortal conclusions, but *affaires d'honneur* were seldom occasioned after the start of the war and ceased entirely once Dragonierre opened his fencing gallery over on 10th and Main and invited gentlemen to settle their scores in less deadly fashion "AT ANY TIME, DAY OR NIGHT!" Courage seemed to be leaking out of our nobles like black bile from a punctured spleen. By March, the number of petitions for substitutes outnumbered those beseeching aid in tracking down escaped Negroes. I do not blame them, I suppose (nor for that matter the runaway slaves); if I were wealthy I might have done the same, had my brother's errant axefall not rendered me *de facto* unfit, but I do question the wisdom of advertising one's cowardice to the general public. If the Confederacy had not finally outlawed the practice later that year, the war might have ended much sooner for sheer lack of men to fight it.

The explosion at the munitions laboratory on Brown's Island was still raw in the public mind at the time, though the wounds of the survivors had healed as much as Mother Nature could muster.

It is hard to imagine a worse blow to the our city's morale than thirty dead daughters and nearly two score more left burned and scarred beyond recognition. Several days after the accident I tried to locate Mary Ryan, the young Irish girl who precipitated the tragedy by banging too hard on a cannon primer, but her parents refused to let me see her. Poor Mary died a few days later. I did succeed in interviewing Cornelia Mitchell at General Hospital No. 2, and shall never forget the hellish light that blazed in her one unscalded eye as it seared me through her veil of gauze. The incessant moaning of the other victims testified to the unbearable pain they were enduring, but Ms. Mitchell seemed intent to suffer in silence. I asked her to describe the moments after the explosion and she focused her eye on a point somewhere over my head and said she would rather not, thank you. With a little more cajoling and sympathetic murmuring I learned that she was not among the dozen or so who ran towards the river, but instead broke off—pell mell and still ablaze—in the direction of the main munitions depot and almost certainly would have annihilated everyone not already killed in the initial detonation had a clearer thinking foreman not tackled her in time. It is exactly this sort of detail that I seek when I settle on a topic—the kind that linger in the mind long after the general particulars fade. Should I fail to find one in fact, I am not above growing my own in fiction's fertile soil. So long as the result does not slander any otherwise upstanding citizen or steal away a story's essential truth, then I feel no guilt in doing so. That being said, the following account neither requires nor would brook even the smallest degree of elaboration. It is—every word of it—the God's honest truth.

One of my duties at the *Dispatch* was to generate the Amusements column that catalogued the various and sundry entertainments available and occasionally to write reviews of the same. Those of lesser means or greater dignity might be surprised to learn that large numbers of ladies and gentlemen continued throughout the war to regularly attend frivolities like Buckley and Company's Southern Nightingale Opera & Farce Troupe or the juvenile antics of Rascal Tim. The New Richmond Theater had just opened in February that year and by all accounts its seats were nearly full for every performance. Perhaps the distraction helped ease anxieties about marauding Yanks. How else to explain the popularity of mechanized falderal like Lee Mallory's "Pantechnoptomon" which commanded standing room attendance at Metropolitan Hall, and which proudly and boldly depicted:

JACKSON CROSSING THE POTOMAC!
Also, the Scenic-Automatic Spectacle of
CAMP AND FIELD LIFE IN VIRGINIA,
And that wonder of mechanical skill,
THE WOUNDED OFFICER and his FAITHFUL HORSE!

With such ample doses of real-life bloodshed delivered daily to their very doorsteps, it is more than curious that our supposed betters found the stomach to seek out more, however abstracted and defanged by melodramatic accoutrement. Additional proof, I suppose, that we are all morbid creatures at heart. And yet I must admit that there is something undeniable about the way a simulacrum can seize the mind and play wondrous tricks on one's sense of reality. In my youth I had often heard tell of the time when Johann Mälzel brought his famous automaton chess master to our fair city and vexed all who witnessed it, including no less a mind than that of our unfortunate Mr. Poe. Early in my career I was able to witness in Philadelphia the exhibition of Joseph Faber's Euphonia, and have been haunted ever since by the memory of that otherworldly voice emanating from a disembodied head. Yet even those masterful contrivances pale in comparison to the miraculous nightmare of Philus Eisen.

I'll never know to whom I owe my introduction. A scrap of paper was left on my desk one day bearing, in nearly illegible scrawl, a simple admonition: *You will not want to miss the show tonight at The Very Bottom.* I am not ashamed to admit I knew the place. As a single man, with normal needs, I did occasionally dip my pen into some of Shockoe's public women, but more often satisfied myself with a bawdy performance, which is exactly what, under normal circumstances, would have been offered that night at this particular establishment. And so it was with severely misguided expectations that I sauntered down to the corner of Twelfth and Arch, where The Very Bottom squatted unsteadily over the canal on its mossy brick haunches like a lady making water. Something about the scene immediately struck me as more perverted than usual. I had acquired a tincture of McMunn's Opium Elixir from my apothecary neighbor, as I found a few drops helped me enjoy the shows without the lingering discomfort of unspent lust, so initially I blamed the distorting effects of the narcotic but the more I looked the more I noticed that none of the normal gaiety attended the men—and it was all men, no couples, temporary or otherwise—who instead stood morosely in line awaiting entry, heads down or hidden behind hats pulled tight. A small placard had been posted by the entrance that read in sum:

Philus Eisen,

The Rememberist

I found my place in the queue and wondered aloud who had died, which earned me several gloomy stares from my peers. It was only then that I detected the source of my disquiet in the odd demographics of the men around me. *Fully one in four lacked a limb.* Most wanted an arm and had sleeves pinned to coats which cleverly hid their deficiency, but I also noted at least two men on crutches with missing legs. The sight of men diminished by their service was no rarity by then, but never so many in one place. As if harkened, a phantom pain rejoined from the two missing fingers on my right hand and I crammed the hand even deeper than usual into my pocket to quiet it. Then the doors opened, we paid our fare and we were let inside.

Absent were the two-bit pianist and the jaunty prelude that normally greeted me as I entered the dingy old theater. In their place was a tense and somber silence. Instead of lantern footlights, tall candlesticks lined the stage with a flickering glow. The sparse crowd took their seats and in short order the show began.

An old man in a surgeon's smock wheeled a gurney onstage that supported a younger gentleman with dark curly hair. A tarp had been laid down and the old man positioned the gurney on top. From a shelf on the bottom he retrieved a black leather satchel and laid it on the gurney. From inside the satchel he withdrew a clamping tourniquet apparatus, a long thin knife, and a bone saw with an ivory grip. He then wrapped the tourniquet around the upper right arm of the man on the gurney, inserted the end through the buckle, pulled it taught, and tightened the clamp with multiple twists. His preparations apparently complete, the old man stepped aside and the man on the gurney addressed the audience.

"What you are about to see is a recreation of a field hospital amputation from March of last year, during the first engagement at Kernstown. Private William Attison of the 5th Virginia Cavalry lost most of his right bicep muscle to a Minié ball. It was quickly decided that the arm must be removed to save Private Attison's life. It was one of three such operations that day."

Without further adieu, the old man ambled back to the gurney, picked up the knife and made several quick incisions. As he leaned over the patient, it was impossible to see exactly what was happening but blood was soon trickling down the gurney and pooling on the tarp. My breath caught short in my throat and I swiveled my head to gauge the reaction of my peers and help determine exactly what I witnessing, but the few around me looked on with stone faces. The old man then stepped back and allowed us to see what he had done.

A flap of the younger's man skin had been cut and peeled back to reveal the raw pink muscle beneath. The old man turned back to his charge and again made quick work with his knife. Another pause and some dabbing with gauze to show us the severed muscle and the white of the bone and again the man on the gurney addressed us, his breathing a bit labored but otherwise under control.

"We require two volunteers from the audience."

I leaked an involuntary laugh at the absurd request, but arms shot up all around me and all of a sudden I remembered that I was attending a performance and the thorned vine of revulsion that had been growing up my spine blossomed into rapt fascination. I raised my arm, sheepishly at first, but then with all the avidity of tack-sharp schoolchild. Had I not been chosen that night I might have limited to that one memorable encounter my exposure to the cursed Mr. Eisen, but life has a curious way of giving us what we think we need. The old man pointed to me and another man and up to the stage I went. I expected to be less convinced of the conceit the closer I approached, but the opposite proved true and in short order I was staring down into the man's carven sinew like a mesmerist's marionette.

"Hold my shoulders firmly please. And do not let go."

The younger man's voice snapped me back to task and I placed my hands on his shoulders as directed. "Harder," he growled. I looked down to see that he was staring me straight in the face with a delirious intensity, his jaw muscles pulsing behind clenched teeth, lips pulled back like a cornered tomcat. I bore down on his shoulders with all my weight, pinning him to the gurney. My cohort did the same with his wrist.

Then the old man began to saw.

Between the sound of the steel abrading the bone and the bucking convulsions of the victim beneath me I very nearly lost control of my senses, but the whole operation was over in a minute. My fellow assistant had been holding so firmly onto the arm in question that he fell over backwards when it was riven and he landed on his rear end with the severed appendage in his lap. He shivered it up and away from him as if it might strike, and then he scrambled away in mortal fear. The old man calmly picked up the arm and displayed it to the audience like a rabbit he had produced from a hat. Then he placed it on the shelf beneath the gurney and began to apply a bandage to the wound.

"You can let up now," said the man beneath me. I looked at him and for a second I was afraid to set him free. But there was a deranged zeal in his eyes and I recoiled as I realized he had not uttered a single cry or moan. The old man supported his torso and helped steady him upright through a period of apparent lightheadedness. Blood was leaking thickly from the stump and soaking the bandage despite the tourniquet and I wondered why the wound had been left unsutured. From somewhere beneath his smock the old man produced a plug of tobacco and handed it to his patient, who inserted it in his gum with his remaining hand. Then the one-armed man addressed the audience.

"Private Attison survived the surgery but succumbed to infection and fever eleven days later. Tonight's performance is dedicated to his memory. One week from tonight, we will remember the fate of Corporal Anders, of Company E."

With that the man bowed, lay back on the gurney, and his partner wheeled him off the stage.

Absolutely nothing about the proceedings smacked of trickery. If anything, I felt it lacked a modicum of showmanship. Several years earlier, as research for a story on the booming market for cadavers, I had attended an autopsy at the Medical College of Virginia. Excepting the use of a live subject, the show that night bore a remarkable resemblance. Immediately I knew that I must speak to Eisen and glean his purpose for mutilating himself. So as the others in the crowd filed out, I made my way to the stage door and knocked. When it became clear that no response was forthcoming, I tried the knob and found it unlocked. Down a dim hallway I found an empty dressing room and another unlocked door that deposited me back outside, in an alley opposite the theater's entrance, at the foot of some steps. Up these steps, I knew, was a one-room flat. It is unimportant why I knew this, for it has no bearing on the present matter, but suffice it to say that I also knew there was a bed in this apartment, that it creaked something awful, and that it's creaking had a distracting habit of animating the roaches in residence. In any case, I climbed those steps and at the top found yet another door not only unlocked but slightly ajar. Through the crack I saw the aforementioned bed and next to it the dismembered man lying on his back in a pine box filled with dark and loamy earth, with only his head above. For a second I thought him dead but the patch of dirt on his chest rose and fell with the rhythm of his breathing. Transfixed by this charnel tableau, I stood staring through the crack until a wizened face appeared in the door and nearly stopped my heart.

"I'm... a reporter with *The Dispatch*," I stammered. "I wish to speak with that man."

The old man gave me nothing in return but his inscrutable regard. He stood mute and immobile as a telamon.

"Come back next week," said the man in the box, as if half asleep. "Find me in the bar before the show." Then the door was closed in my face.

That week lasted longer than some entire years of my life, and it proved impossible to work. I busied myself trying to ascertain who had left me the note but no one at the paper would admit to it, nor did anyone seem to know the first thing about any unusual performances being staged in the city. Friday rolled around at last, and all day I felt gloomily certain I had seen the last of Eisen but no, there he was sitting at the bar at The Very Bottom, gripping a glass of whiskey with the very same hand on the very same arm I had seen sawn off with my very own eyes. He looked up at me as I approached and he reached out with the arm in question wearing a slightly pixilated smile on his face.

"Philus Eisen," he said, shaking my hand. His grip was limp and a disagreeable softness in the texture of his palm triggered a quick retraction on my part. I introduced myself, and gave my professional credentials. He invited me to sit with him and have a whiskey, which he acquired with a word to the bartender, who complied but seemed unable or unwilling to look Eisen in the face. I can understand why. It is hard to put into words, but Eisen looked *ruined* somehow. Like a mongrel dog beaten beyond the capacity for loyalty, or a young war widow forced to remarry for support. And yet, amid the forced laughter of the whores and all those God-fearing men getting loudly and unabashedly drunk, the events of the Friday before seemed but a midnight delusion washed away in morning light.

"So it was a trick?"

"No."

"Pardon me, an *illusion.*"

"No I say."

"I don't understand."

"Neither do I."

"So you sewed it back on? Your partner must be the greatest surgeon in history."

"Bastian? He butchered my hogs before the war..." Eisen seemed to drift off a moment in reverie, as if he had forgotten I was there. His face softened and for a very brief time whatever darkness he carried with him seemed to lift. Then, like a shutter dropping, the shade was upon him again and he fixed me with a cruel stare.

"I feed them to his dogs, actually. They have quite a taste for it by now."

I sipped my whiskey and digested the implications of *them* and *it*.

"I give up then. Am I supposed to believe that you sprouted a new arm?"

He unbuttoned his shirt sleeves and rolled them back. Then he displayed the bare arms to me in tandem. The left was matted with mature black hairs, and had sinewy contours suggesting muscles and tendons beneath. The right was soft, hairless, and nearly translucent, like the grub of a June bug.

"Fascinating," I stated, for it was, but it was also nauseating.

"Look closer," he invited. I leaned in as he laid the arm atop the bar. I could not be certain, for the light in the place was not sufficient, but it seemed as if the arm was growing incrementally more material and less like a thing unearthed from a subterranean lake. I described it as hairless, for I swear it was just moments before, but as I watched a few thin hairs broke through his pores and thickened into life.

I raised my hand and ordered another whiskey.

"Make it a double."

I turned back to my companion, who was staring at me with that same queer smile on his face. I mistook him for drunk, but another kind of mischief was at work behind his eyes. I noticed then that his shirt collar was open and that snaking around his neck was a jagged pink scar. He saw where my eyes had drawn and raised the back of that foetal hand to rub the scar and seemed ready to speak, but something over my shoulder caught his eye. I followed his gaze to find Bastian standing in a doorway behind the bar and the utterly emotionless way the old man nodded to Eisen filled me with a terrible foreboding.

"Enjoy the show," Philus laughed and rose from his seat. "It's on me." As he passed me he pressed a chit into my hand. Then he followed Bastian through the door.

I am thankful for two reasons that I did not volunteer to aid in the performance that night. For one, it would have ruined my career, if not my reputation. For another, I am not certain I would have left the stage with my mind intact. The few minutes with Eisen in the bar had left me feeling like a storm was fast approaching and brief flashes of lightning were firing off in the distance and silhouetting the shape of something monstrous on the horizon.

"Tonight we remember Lieutenant Corporal Grayson Anders, a graduate of the Albermarle Military Institute and member of Company H, 13th Tennessee Infantry. While bravely serving at

Shiloh, Corporal Anders had the misfortune of having his left foot and lower leg crushed by cannon recoil. There was little choice but to remove the damaged segment."

Eisen again remained silent as his assistant sawed off his left leg just above the knee. The operation took longer this time and required more force. At one point Bastion had to employ a vicious looking pair of snips to cut through some tougher sections of the femur. Towards the end, one of the men holding Eisen down fainted dead away. He was left where he fell for there were more pressing matters at hand. Instead of watching the action, which was, quite frankly, beginning to sicken me, I chose to focus on the fallen man. He came around in a minute or two and after he sat up he began to rub his brow incessantly as if a blot or stain there, somewhere just behind his forehead, demanded instant removal. Eventually conceding failure, he rose unsteadily to his feet and exited the building without looking back. I wish with all my heart that I had summoned the good sense to do the same.

After the operation was complete, Eisen invited the audience to approach the stage and inspect the severed leg while Bastian packed the wound with rags. Only a few obliged, but they did so with the wide-eyed reverence of pilgrims. It was while these men were recessing back to their seats that a commotion erupted at the back of the theater. I swiveled my head to see a company of police officers barge in and march down the aisle. Two of them climbed the stage, immediately bent Bastian and the remaining volunteer over the gurney and put them in handcuffs. Eisen had somehow managed to get down and I saw Captain Weaver grab him as he tried to drag himself to the stage door. Weaver knew me a little and liked me less and I crouched down in my seat in the hope of hiding my face. The other police began to usher the small crowd from the theater. I joined the exodus and kept my head down but just before the door I looked back at the stage. Eisen was still struggling mightily to escape and Weaver was beating him down with a billy club. The severed leg still sat at the stage lip, seemingly unnoticed.

By all rights that should have ended my gruesome little affair with Eisen but a few days later I got word at the office that I was wanted by Captain Weaver at Chimborazo. I hailed a coach to the recently completed hospital, way out on the East end of town, just past the city line. It was my first visit and, despite the circumstances, I found myself marveling at the massive network of individual wards built on a forty-acre plateau across from Bloody Run Creek. One of Weaver's deputies met me at the gate and escorted me to a building at the back of the hospital, at the far end of a single row of wards running perpendicular to and set off from the main grid. The deputy walked me to the door and then stood to the side at attention with another guard. Inside I found Eisen in bed looking pale and gazing morosely out the window. A sheet covered him to the waist, but I could tell by its asymmetrical drape that he still lacked a leg. Weaver was facing Eisen, in a chair by the bed, but he stood as I entered and took me outside. We nodded at one another but did not shake hands.

"I extended you a courtesy, Harlan, by not sending one of my men for you and embarrassing you at your place of employment, but my well of good graces is only so deep. I need to know the nature of your relationship with this man."

"I have none."

"He says otherwise. In fact, he patently refuses to speak to anyone but you."

"I am not sure what help I can be, Captain. We spoke briefly at a bar last night. He introduced himself as Philus Eisen."

"Impossible."

For a second I thought that Weaver was calling me a liar.

"Eisen died in Castle Thunder over a year ago."

I raised my eyebrows at the mention of the infamous prison but said nothing.

"Against my better judgment I am prepared to make a deal with you Harlan. I want you to interview this man and see what you can find out. When I am finished with him you can use whatever you want in one of your *columns*." He spat the last word as if it tasted of manure.

I had little choice but to comply, but room enough to protect myself.

"He won't talk with you in the room."

Weaver had anticipated me and was already walking away, "If he tells you anything at all, I expect a full report." I started towards the door. "I'm leaving my men here to keep an eye on you both," the Captain threw back at me as he departed.

Eisen was still staring out the window when I came back inside.

"Byrd wasn't far from here when he named Richmond."

I settled into the chair and took out my notebook. "Is that so?"

Eisen nodded, still not looking at me. "There's a spot a little ways up, where the topography mirrors a bend in the Thames near our city's namesake. Funny how we hope to make a thing familiar by just giving it a familiar name."

"And your namesake, this Eisen fellow, what made you want to take the name of a criminal?"

"I took nothing. Criminal or not, he is I and I am him."

"Weaver says Eisen died at Castle Thunder."

"And so he did," Eisen conceded. A weariness had overcome him. "I know what you're after Harlan, and I am prepared to give it to you, but you must do something for me first."

It was fortunate for me that they had put Eisen by himself in a building set off the rest, for no one had a vantage to witness me climb through the window with an empty sack from the ward's linen closet and begin filling it with earth. I felt the insanity of what I was doing, whether folly or sorcery, but it was too late to turn back now. I climbed back over the sill and helped Eisen secure the bag around his stump with his belt. Afterwards he leaned back with a sigh, and then he began to speak. His tale was long and meandering, and the deeper into it he got the more he sounded like a madman. I include here the gist of what I eventually communicated to Captain Weaver.

When the war broke, Eisen was a general physician serving a small community in Midlothian. Johan, his younger brother, of whom he was extremely fond, decided to enlist. When he died at Bull Run from what Eisen later determined was the shoddy treatment of a relatively minor wound, Eisen realized his services were desperately needed.

"I thought I could save them all," he said simply, palms up.

So he joined up in late '61 and at first he just ministered to those brought back to Richmond, but his skill did not go unnoticed and soon enough he was moved to the front lines. He was present at Kernstown and Fort Donelson, and when at Shiloh he saw what a field looked like littered with ten thousand dead, he basically lost his mind.

"Do you know what a cannon ball does to a line of human beings?" Eisen asked of me. "Bodies upon bodies... piles of bodies... torn to pieces and jumbled together like offal. Like a leviathan sickle had swept through the men and reaped their tasty bits."

He continued to serve, continued to saw off limbs and save what few lives he could, but at some point in the spring of '62 he became obsessed with the notion of effecting an end to the war.

"My people didn't have slaves or plantations to protect. All I saw was young men dying in numbers enough to invoke the Apocalypse."

On the evening of June 25, 1862, at the outset of the Seven Days, with Union forces nearly knocking on the city gates, Eisen concocted a daring but foolish plan to sneak across to the enemy and personally deliver to General McClellan a list of troop strengths and positions that had fallen into his hands during a meeting with senior officers trying to allot triage units accordingly.

Eisen knew, along with everyone else, that if Richmond fell then the entire Confederacy would soon follow. He was captured en route, however, and a search uncovered enough evidence to take him into custody. He did not help matters by trying to convince his captors to join him in treason.

According to Eisen, being sent to Castle Thunder while he awaited trial was a natural progression in his own private *Inferno*, and for certain his descriptions of the prison made it sound like nothing less than the ninth circle of hell. I myself had, on more than one occasion, stood outside the imposing old tobacco warehouse on Cary and wondered what sort of fiendish treatment was accorded the low men housed within. I never lingered long, though, for the guards took unkindly to anyone paying too much attention.

Eisen told me that in addition to all the spies, traitors, and prisoners of war, Castle Thunder also housed an invisible population of evil men no other facility cared to contain—soldiers who had, either in the course of their service or its tormented wake, committed acts heinous enough to revoke their right to due process and were thereby kept hidden from the attention of the press and the general populace.

"Such as?" I interrupted. God help me, I had to know.

Eisen waved away the question and then answered it anyway. "Infanticide. Battlefield necrophilia. Trophy collecting of the most revolting sort imaginable."

Eisen called these men demons and it was his belief, which I found credible given the other despicable charges publicly leveled at Commandant Alexander, that the guards used these inhumans as their personal thugs, to enforce rules and deliver punishments. In Eisen's case, they evidently went beyond the pale and actually embodied the demonic beings he took them to be.

Everyone in the prison knew that Eisen had served as a field surgeon and what that meant he had done in the name of medicine. They also knew he had attempted to hand Richmond to the North. Many of his fellow traitors came to him for whatever doctoring he could muster and Eisen was able to survive while other men starved thanks to their miniscule payments of bread and broth. But a handful of the demons had fallen under the saw and they did not thank their surgeons, but instead blamed them for their whole cursed existence and whatever sins they had committed to get there. Two such fiends named Blount and Cobham took a special interest in Eisen and harassed him mercilessly with help from their cohorts until they bored of petty tortures. One dark night in a fit of blood lust they descended on Eisen, hung him to within an inch of death and then cut off his arms and legs.

Eisen delivered this denouement with the same nonchalance exhibited above and for a moment I thought his whole account was an elaborate dido.

"What do you mean they cut off your arms and legs?"

"Exactly that. The demons understood only the most medieval definition of justice and so they decreed that for my crimes against king and country I must be drawn and quartered. They stripped me naked and strung me up in the prison basement using a length of the barbed wire that kept us from scaling the fence."

Here Eisen paused and displayed the jagged scar I had noticed that night in the bar.

"Lacking a horse to drag me around with or a blade to disembowel me, they simply took turns using the barbed wire like a rope saw until I was nothing but a torso lying in a pool of my own blood."

I stared at Eisen a moment, unable to speak, silently beseeching his face for some hint of deception. "And then?"

"And then the guards found me and tossed me into a shallow grave in the potter's field behind the prison."

"And then?"

Eisen looked at me blankly, shrugged, and shook his head. He opened his mouth to speak, inhaled sharply, and then just shook his head again. He had no answer, no explanation. Instead he lifted the sheet from his stump, loosened the belt around the bag of earth, and invited me to look inside.

Mr. Valdemar

Beth Brown

It was a damp November morning when I got the call from my dear friend, Mr. Valdemar. His doctors had given him a grim prognosis – pancreatic cancer, aggressive, and definitely terminal. They expected that he only had two weeks left, maybe less.

I met Mr. Valdemar while I was still a psychology student at VCU, shortly before entering the Pre-Med program. He was teaching then, but when he discovered that we shared an interest in psychical phenomena, particularly the powers of mind-over-matter, he took it upon himself to strike up the occasional debate. Perhaps it was because I could hold my own end of the argument, or perhaps it was simply that I took his challenges seriously that sparked our longtime friendship. Even after I earned my credentials and he retired from teaching over twenty years ago, I would often answer my phone to find Mr. Valdemar on the other end with some amazing question or theory. Today, though, there was only his request to come talk with him at his bedside about the future of our studies together.

I had been to his house a few times over the years, and during those visits I had never stepped foot out of the first-floor parlor. When I knocked at the door that morning, a hospice nurse greeted me and escorted me directly to the third floor without saying a word. I stepped into what looked like a library, shelves of leather-bound books lined the walls and stacks of dusty volumes were perched on nearly every horizontal surface, to see my old friend lying in a brass bed in the center of the room.

Though Mr. Valdemar and I had met for lunch only a few weeks earlier, he looked as if he had aged another decade in the interim. His face had grown thin and his cheeks were sunken in a way that, upon noticing, twists your gut with knowledge of the inevitable. His skin had taken on a grey undertone that I had become far too familiar with, and the white of his teeth seemed unusually prominent in contrast. The signs of death were all around him, yet his eyes were still the same, focused and determined, like they were when we met.

"Come in, Miss Poole. My apologies for the mess," he said. I was unsure if he meant the state of the room or himself, but I dared not question. "I suppose you are wondering why I asked you to visit so urgently? There is a favor I wish you to consider. An odd request from a dying man, but something which I hope you will entertain."

"Of course. What can I do?"

"Help me with an experiment. My final test of the power of the mind, if you will," he answered. "The hospice nurses will be with me all the time during my last days, and when my death is close, one of them will call you to come back. No matter what my state of mind then, and you must promise me this – you are to hypnotize me."

"Okay." I was unsure where he was going with this experiment, and I had never been more curious in all of my life. "And what then?"

"Nothing. Let me stay that way until my moment of passing. I want to go in peace, with my mind independent of pain medication. I know that with your expertise in hypnosis, I could be in no better hands." One corner of his mouth turned up in a hint of a smile and his white whiskers glittered in the sliver of sunlight that shone across the bed. This was the only direct compliment, if you could even call it direct, that Mr. Valdemar had ever paid me. I could tell by the emotion in his eyes, however, that the fondness was not new. "Well, nothing to say?"

"I... I suppose I could do that. But how will I know if the hypnosis has eased your pain?" I replied.

"Just ask me. While you have me out, just ask me what you want to know. You've done this hundreds of times, Poole, don't lapse on professionalism just because it's me you're dealing with." There was the Mr. Valdemar I knew, and he was right. All of my years of hypnotherapy had, by his own admission, fascinated him, but he had never before asked to be the subject of a session. I am not one to deny a dying man his wishes, so I agreed to his plan with a nod. "Right, then," he said and extended a shrunken and pale hand for his usual business-like handshake. I somehow expected the same strength I saw in his eyes and heard in his voice to also be present in that handshake, but my heart sank when I discovered his skin was cold and clammy and his grip nearly gone.

We chatted for a bit and debated a theory or two when I could tell that exhaustion was creeping in for him. I said my good-byes and got up to leave when he said, "Poole, take that stack there by the door. They're for you." The stack to which he referred was a collection of books on a side table, some nearly a century old, on the practice of Mesmerism. I must have worn the astonishment on my face, because when I looked back at Mr. Valdemar, he gave a little wink before closing his eyes to rest.

His hospice nurse told me later that ours was the last conversation Mr. Valdemar had. He slipped into a coma sometime later that afternoon, and his condition then declined almost by the hour.

It was five days after my visit that a nurse called to inform me that Mr. Valdemar had less than a day to go. His heart rate and breathing had slowed so much that they were barely distinguishable, and his color had turned from grey to the tell-tale blue that comes when one arrives at death's door. Within fifteen minutes of receiving the call, I had canceled my remaining appointments of the day and was standing on Mr. Valdemar's front porch in Church Hill.

A nurse let me in and I hung my coat on a hall tree inside the door. The house was incredibly cold, but my nerves were drawing tiny beads of perspiration to my brow. The nurse led me upstairs to the bedroom, where upon entering I found my friend connected to a heart monitor and a bag of intravenous fluids. His skin looked as though no blood flowed beneath its surface, and his sunken cheeks had given way even further, making him look strangely skeletal. Though he was still comatose, his eyes were half-open and, at first glace, he appeared to be merely dozing off. A second nurse was measuring his blood pressure when she looked towards me and said, "Not long now." An ache in my chest snapped me back to the task at hand – fulfilling my mentor's final request.

The nurses moved aside, clearly curious about what I intended to attempt, and allowed me to sit on the edge of the bed. I leaned close to what was left of Mr. Valdemar and said, "I'm here; it's Ellen Poole. I've come like you asked me to." There was a faint flutter of the eyelids just then that caused great excitement in the hospice nurses, but I ignored them as much as possible and continued, "Mr. Valdemar, I'm going to begin the hypnosis now. I want to you to listen very carefully to my voice and try as hard as you can to follow the pendulum with your eyes." His eyes were open only a tiny bit, mere slits, really, and I hoped that he could somehow see me, or else the process would never work.

I reached into my skirt pocket and pulled out the tiny brass disc. Holding it by the fob at the end of its chain, I held it near the dying man's face and started the pendulum's slow, rhythmic movements. Doubt scuttled through my mind at that moment – I had never been able to fully hypnotize Mr. Valdemar in the previous twenty-five years, how on Earth did I expect to manage that feat while he was in this state? After what seemed like hours, I watched his eyes tip up behind the lids, an indicator that my fear may have been premature. Mr. Valdemar had always claimed he had been able to resist hypnosis, but maybe his willingness to accept the process now was a saving grace?

"You are sleeping, Mr. Valdemar. You feel only comfort; no pain. You are calm and relaxed. You are sleeping and you are comfortable. You will remain this way until I say otherwise."

I could not have anticipated the events that followed that moment, nor would I have wanted to, but I assure you that they are the complete truth and were witnessed by eyes and ears other than my own.

Mr. Valdemar's pallor changed from the grey of approaching death to a stark white so void of color that he almost appeared to glow in the dim winter light of the bedroom. His lips withered and shrank while his mouth fell open just enough to glimpse his darkened tongue. A chill came over me just as his entire body began to vibrate, not violently like a seizure, rather like a current of electricity had passed through it. The nurses gasped and one backed away from the bed so rapidly that she nearly injured herself stumbling over stacks of books. With hands over their mouths, their wide eyes looked on with the same horror and disbelief as my own. A sound as hollow as a well and as distant as the horizon emerged from Mr. Valdemar's constricted face:

"I am sleeping... I am dying. No pain. Let me be."

I took Mr. Valdemar's hand in mine and found it cool to the touch. I moved his arm around over his body and was met with no resistance. He appeared to be completely relaxed and comfortable, just as I had instructed. The heart monitor chirped out its tiny beeps like some sort of Chinese water torture, and I realized then that in all of my years of hypnotherapy, no other experience had prepared me for this. A comatose man was fully hypnotized and was responding to my prompts. I looked at the hospice nurses, who exchanged nervous looks and then answered the question asked by my puzzled expression. "I've never seen anything like this before," one said. "I guess all we can do is just let nature take its course now."

The nurses assured me that the end was imminent and that he was not likely to survive the night. They urged me to go home and get some rest, and I agreed after they promised that they would call me as soon as Mr. Valdemar passed.

I busied myself with research for the remainder of the day, but was sure to keep my phone lines free in anticipation of that somber call. Darkness fell, and eventually I tried to sleep, but the bizarre events from earlier that day refused to leave my mind. Replaying over and over were the words spoken by that voice that came from somewhere between the world of the living and the world of the dead. By morning, I was in a cold sweat from the flood of mixed emotions that pounded inside of me, but the phone call never came.

It was barely seven o'clock when a nurse met me at Mr. Valdemar's door. She looked every bit as tired as I did, but had an odd, panicky flit about her that warned me something was off. "How is he?" I asked.

"You should come and see for yourself."

The bedroom was dark, but in the faint light cast by a reading lamp, I could see that Mr. Valdemar was resting as peacefully as when I had left the day before. The heart monitor still measured a pulse, and once I got close enough, I could hear his slow, shallow breathing. "I thought you said he was doing too poorly to last through another night?"

"I'm not sure what to tell you, Miss Poole. He was declining rapidly until, you know, until you paid him a visit. He's just leveled off since then. I've never seen anyone so close to the end hang on for this long," the nurse explained. She shifted her weight from one foot to the other, clearly upset about the present circumstances. I was unsure if the reason for her feelings was because of making a bad prediction or because of what we had witnessed a day earlier, but logic told me that it was more reasonably the latter.

I sat again on the edge of his bed and took his hand in mine.

"Mr. Valdemar, are you still sleeping?" Several minutes passed before there was a noticeable flutter of his eyelids and a slight twitch of his hand. His mouth did not move, but I heard an unusual change in his breathing. It was when I leaned in closer that I noticed the sound coming from his parted lips was a response. My hands started to tremble, but I managed to stutter out, "Please say that again, Mr. Valdemar – I... I couldn't quite hear you." That same hollow voice I had heard the day before returned, this time more distant and chilling.

"I am sleeping; dying. I am nearly dead."

The nurse who had let me in the front door hurried out of the room without saying a word, and the second nurse sat gripping the arms of an old wing chair until her knuckles turned as pale as my old friend's face. I lifted Mr. Valdemar's arm and moved it again back and forth over his body. He was completely relaxed, still fully hypnotized. I looked toward the nurse, "So, I suppose all we can do is wait?" She answered with a shrug.

Reluctantly, I waited. Watching someone die, no matter how peaceful they may appear, is excruciating, but I endured the emotional marathon and stayed at Mr. Valdemar's bedside until late that night. The nurses cared for him by combing his hair and giving him fresh blankets, explaining to me that, as was the usual procedure for someone that close to the end, they would also need to remove his IV. Hours passed, yet he still took slow, quiet breaths. The nurses disconnected the heart monitor around Midnight, and each of us knew that the machine was pointless at this stage and only served to drive us slightly mad with its incessant beeping.

Just when it seemed that time had come to a standstill, I could make out the faint pink light of the approaching dawn. I had never expected my friend to hold on for that long and I had a calendar full of patients scheduled to see me that day. Even without sleep, I knew that I had an obligation to fulfill and another day of cancelation was not an option I could consider. My heart was heavy with the idea of leaving Mr. Valdemar before the end, but I did not know if I could take much more of the waiting. There is a guilt so tremendous that comes along with the hope of seeing a dying man's suffering cease that I do not think I could express it here in words.

The weight of my emotions pushed me to the edge of desperation. I decided to address Mr. Valdemar once more, secretly hoping that this time he would be too far gone to respond. "Mr. Valdemar, it's Miss Poole. Are you still sleeping?" His breaths were very few, and they seemed to come only every minute or two. I had determined then that he didn't have the strength or the recognition left to answer, but that eerie and surreal trembling returned then to his limbs.

"Was sleeping. Now... Now I am dead."

A chill crawled up my arms and left a tingle on my scalp. My brain struggled to comprehend what I had just heard, but the gasp from the two attending nurses and their looks of fear and confusion assured me that it had been no illusion. As we stood there processing the moment, I noticed a change in Mr. Valdemar's face. His paper white skin was suddenly marked by sunken and dark hollows of the cheeks and eyes. His skeletal arms felt cold to the touch, yet moved willingly over his body when guided by my hand, still indicative of hypnosis.

One of the nurses hurried to the bedside with a stethoscope

and placed it under his pajama shirt and against his chest. After a minute of intense listening, she turned to me and said, "There is still a very faint heartbeat, and it's the slowest and strangest thing I've ever heard." We all watched and wondered what was going on inside of the mind of that brilliant but assuredly stubborn man. There were no more ragged breaths, no slight rise and fall of his chest, and his eyes no longer moved about under the lids as they do during sleep. Aside from the odd heartbeat and the words spoken only moments ago, Mr. Valdemar showed every sign of death.

The nurse with the stethoscope placed a hand on my shoulder. "I think it would be okay if you left. We'll stay here with him and monitor his condition. I can't declare him dead or call the funeral home until his heart finally winds down, which I assume will be shortly."

With her reassurance, I went to my office and met with patients. My mind was foggy with the events of the previous forty-eight hours, and I found myself sobbing with a mix of grief and confusion between each appointment. That dark emotional state hung over me for the next seven months. It did not take me that length of time for me to grieve for Mr. Valdemar – it took that length of time for Mr. Valdemar to truly die.

The drive from my office at the Medical College to his Church Hill home was a short one, and I made the trip every day after work to check on my friend. I think it took me all those months to realize that the Mr. Valdemar I had known was really gone, and all that was left was an empty shell to remind me of what I had done. Why had he asked me to do such a thing? Hypnotize a dying man!

I should have known better, but the gnawing of curiosity was too great. There was no curiosity left in me then, only regret.

A rotation of hospice nurses still kept watch at his bedside even though there was no natural explanation of his condition. No IV had been reconnected, no breathing assistance had been offered, and yet he remained frozen in time – yet his heart still twitched.

That day in June, less than a week from Mr. Valdemar's birthday, I decided what needed to be done. I don't know if it was fear, guilt, or a perverted sense of responsibility that had kept me from doing it sooner, but I eventually summoned the strength to complete the deed. I informed the nursing staff of my intentions, and (I suspect purely out of morbid fascination) they had four nurses in attendance that afternoon.

I sat at the edge of his bed like I always did, took his cold hand in mine and tested his movement as usual. He was still and relaxed, yet his arm moved freely with my guidance. "Mr. Valdemar, it's Miss Poole. I think the time has come for us to end our experiment." I took a deep breath to steady my nerves. "Listen carefully, friend. When I snap my fingers three times, you will be released from your trace." The nurses gathered around closely, examining my every move. I placed Mr. Valdemar's hand on his chest and I stood beside his head. Holding my fingers close to his ear, I gently made the promised three snaps.

It was at that moment that the room seemed to spin. Time turned thick and everything I witnessed after the snapping of my fingers felt as if it happened in slow motion. One nurse ran from the room, and I suspect directly out the front door. Another swooned while the remaining two covered their stretched and terrified mouths with their hands. I'm not sure if I had only imagined it, but I remember the strange sensation of the air being sucked from the room in an audible whoosh.

In front of me, lying on the bed, was a grotesque and putrid mass of liquid and bone. Where moments before had been white skin and silvery whiskers, there now rested a slick yellow film. Where once were peaceful sleeping eyelids, there now stared vacant sockets.

Seven months of death and decay, postponed for too long, had arrived in an instant.

The Third Office

Dale Brumfield

Billy Bendix peered over the seeming acre of dark blue sheet metal between him and the road from the driver's seat of father-in-law's spotless Crown Victoria, reminding him of sitting at the beach looking across the ocean. "My gosh, what a car." he muttered, admiring the expansive comfort. "You got the directions, Hazy?"

"They're right here," his wife Hazel answered as she unfolded a sheet of lined notebook paper and studied her own scribbled handwriting. "We take Interstate 64 west to the Staples Mill exit, then take a left off Staples Mill to a feeder road behind the Amtrak station, then take another road . . ."

"What other road? Be more specific – I don't know where this place is."

"Don't get smart!" Hazel snapped, "This guy Howard something who called talked so fast I had trouble writing the directions. But I did make him say twice we were guaranteed to win either a 2011 Yukon or $5,000.00 cash just for showing up and touring this place!"

After exiting the highway and then turning off of Staples Mill Road, Hazel squinted at her handwriting, hoping the name would just pop out at her. "Sump, Rump, Bump Road" she muttered out loud as Billy slowed down to read the jumble of confusing signs on a hidden gravel road somewhere beyond the train tracks.

"Stump Road" he suddenly said, pointing to a crooked road sign among a cluster of others, "Think that's it?"

"Gotta be." Hazel agreed, relieved as Billy hooked onto the narrow alley. "Go three miles south, then merge left at the fork, go to the third stop sign at an empty warehouse park, turn left I think, then follow signs to landfill . . ."

"Landfill?" Billy blurted, "A resort located on a landfill? In Richmond? It's sounding more classy all the time!"

"I'm sure it's not actually on a landfill," Hazel said. "Who builds an exclusive time-share resort on a landfill?"

They drove around the dead industrial park for several minutes until finally they passed a weedy vacant lot with a giant, faded "Landfill" sign with the owner's name blacked out. Underneath was a sheet of plywood with a crude spray-painted arrow pointing further down the road that read "Resort this way".

After a few more minutes they finally saw a large sandblasted sign in the shape of a brick Georgian mansion reading "Welcome to LaFontanel. An Ultra-Premium Resort Community".

Sighing with relief Billy turned the huge car onto the recently asphalted entryway, rounded a bend and came upon a large, two-story Greek-style brick and vinyl-sided clubhouse. Idle construction equipment littered the ground.

After parking they entered the front double-doors of a clubhouse decorated in garish Louis XIV filigree that looked more at home in a French bordello than a cheesy time-share resort.

"Are you here for the tour?" asked a heavyset man with a bad comb-over and a sweaty shirt behind the welcome counter as he flipped through a stack of index cards. "I mean, were you invited or did you wander in? We get a lot of street trash here."

"We're not street trash, we were invited." Billy said. "You called us. The name is Bendix."

"Ah-ha – Billy and Hazel?" the man extended his white, pudgy hand. "Welcome to LaFontanel Ultra-Premium Time-Share Resorts Worldwide!" he said, suddenly very chipper. "My name is Howard DeRoach. I believe we spoke on the phone, Mrs. Bendix?"

Hazel shook DeRoach's hand first. It was cold and sweaty. "I trust you had a safe trip here." he motioned with his sweaty hand. "Let's start your presentation, shall we?"

DeRoach led them up some steps into a sparsely appointed office with a gold number 1 on the door. "Mr. Bleasdale is our top marketing rep," Howard said as he closed the door, "he will be right with you". Billy and Hazel sat down, but before they had a chance to even catch their breath the door suddenly opened again and an obese black man in a shiny suit and reeking of cheap after-shave waddled in. As the door closed he stopped dramatically.

"My name is Happy Bleasdale." he said as he walked behind the desk, hiked up his pants, took deliberate aim at his chair with his large polyester butt and slid down, pushing all the air out of the vinyl seat cushion with a furious, extended *br-fraaapp!* sound. "Do you folks know why I'm so happy? Spending two weeks' vacation every year for practically pennies, thanks to LaFontanel's patented exclusive Payments in Perpetuity program! That's what makes me so happy!"

A very smug and self-satisfied man, Happy leaned back and

folded his arms over his head before he abruptly sat forward as his seat went *blorp!* "Folks, with deeded property like a house, you make payments for ten to thirty years. What do you get for your money? I'll tell you what you get – bills. More money you have to shell out. You make those high monthly mortgage payments and what do you get in return?

"Shelter," Hazel answered, "A home. Memories . . ."

Happy made a face. *Blurp!* "Family, shelter – yea, that's nice but happy memories don't pay the bills! It's all about the money! Electric, gas, water and sewer bills – they actually charge you for going to the bathroom! It's a terrible, endless cycle. Plus, if it's memories you're after, believe me when your kids are all grown up they will cherish not some old house but the fabulous vacations taken at LaFontanel's exclusive worldwide resorts!"

Happy pulled a stack of 8-1/2" x 11" photos out of his top desk drawer. "With LaFontanel time-share resort properties' patented exclusive payments in perpetuity program, we've taken all the worry out of monthly installments." *Frump!*

He showed a picture of a gorgeous, beautifully decorated condominium, obviously cut from a magazine. "You make the minimum 51% down payment on one of our luxurious, tastefully decorated deeded units, then you make low, low monthly payments not for ten, twenty, thirty years, but for the rest of your life, and for the rest of your children's lives – or, for seventy years after your death, whichever comes first."

The next card showed a standard stock-art photo of a smiling retired couple on some beach. "Then LaFontanel purchases the property back from you or your heirs at fair market value . . . in cold cash!" Card number three was a big dollar sign. "One easy payment every month, in perpetuity, that's it. No bills. And in return you get membership in the LaFontanel family of two-star resorts worldwide, which enables you and your heirs to stay in any of our 127 luxurious properties practically any two weeks of the year for practically pennies!"

Suddenly Bleasdale lay down the cards, leaned forward and scowled at the young couple. "But do you know what makes me *really* happy?"

Timed exactly with Bleasdale's sudden personality change Hazel became aware of a dark and sinister presence in the room that like an octopus arm slithered out of nowhere and softly curled around her shoulder as a hideous chemical odor reached her nose. She shifted uncomfortably and started to look down when. . .

"Holy crap!"

Actually, Billy was the one who saw it a split second before Hazel did. It was gnarled, long and grey, slithering around Hazel's left upper arm, moving slowly and deliberately until Billy yelled and it snapped away. Terrified, Billy and Hazel both jumped to their feet and turned, confronting a hideous, stooped giant of a man standing behind them.

"It's OK folks," Bleasdale quickly said, "This is Mr. Nimrod, President and CEO of LaFontanel Ultra-Premium Resort Properties Worldwide! He's paying you a special visit!"

Mr. Nimrod was the most freakish and gruesome gargoyle of a man Hazel and Billy had ever seen. Scraping the ceiling at almost eight feet in height, his head was a balding skull stretched in pale, translucent skin. He had large, yellowish bulging eyes, thin, pale lips stretched into a leering grin and a huge, blooming tracheotomy hole at the base of his throat. He wore a stained white shirt and Goodwill sport coat with the right sleeve torn away to accommodate his grisly arm, which was more an independently-moving tentacle. His overall person was so ghastly, disturbing, and stinking of rotten garbage that Hazel had to put her hand to her nose and convince herself she was looking at a human being and not a horror movie prop.

As Billy and Hazel stood dumbstruck at the half-human beast before them, Mr. Nimrod raised a little black voice box up with his left hand and held it flat against the center of his throat under his huge, bobbing adam's apple.

"DIDN'T-MEAN-TO-STARTLE-YOU-FOLKS" he said in a spooky robotic voice through the hole in his throat. He smiled eerily, displaying a row of tiny yellow pointed teeth set in black gums.

"Mr. and Mrs. Bendix were just getting ready to sign up, Mr. Nimrod!" Bleasdale said gleefully.

"HAPPY-TREATING-YOU-FOLKS-OK"

"Um he's been just fine . . . whoops!" Hazel ducked as Mr. Nimrod's elephant man right arm suddenly flopped within inches of her face. Clutching his voice box, Nimrod grabbed his flailing right arm with his left and held it still as he peered almost lasciviously down at Hazel, gesturing for them to sit back down.

"I-JUST-CAME-FROM-OUR-GRAND-PRIZE-DRAW-*OW DAMMIT*" Nimrod said, trying to look casual after whacking his own ear with his renegade arm. "YOU-FOLKS-ARE-IN-FOR-A-PLEASANT-SURPRISE"

Billy turned to face Nimrod. The stink slapped him in the face. "Did we win the car or the cash?"

Nimrod winked at Hazel then turned to Bleasdale. "KEEP-UP-THE-GOOD-WORK-HAPPY-   I'LL-SEE-THE-BENDIX-FAMILY-LATER-WHEN-THEY-ARE-READY-TO-SIGN-A-LEASE"

Nimrod ducked way, way down to clear the door as his elephantine right arm flailed and smacked the wall with a thud, knocking off a framed picture. Billy picked it up, noticing in it Howard DeRoach smiling at the camera as he pushed a golden shovel into the ground. A tag at the bottom read "Groundbreaking for LaFontanel Resort, October 31, 2007".

"It was . . . nice meeting you." Hazel said in a faltering voice as Nimrod finally cleared the room and shut the door, leaving only his chemical stink behind.

"There goes a real Renaissance man," Happy said, oblivious to the strangling odor in the room. "He built this resort from the ground up. Well folks, if you have no more questions you need to go see my associate Mr. Samson in office number 2 to complete the next step in your time-share journey."

Still stunned by Nimrod's appearance, Hazel and Billy stood and opened the door only to bump into Howard DeRoach standing just outside in the hall, sweating more than normal.

"Oh! Um, did Mr. Bleasdale complete your, uh . . ."

"Did you just have your ear against the door?" Billy asked as he walked out.

"What? Are you serious?"

"Your ear is flaming red," Hazel pointed out, "Were you

listening in on us?"

"No!" Howard sputtered as he turned and walked quickly toward the next office. "I did no such thing!"

Howard continued to deny eavesdropping as he led them into the second office. "Please, have a seat," he said, eager to change the subject as he dabbed his moist forehead. "Mr. Samson will be right with you to describe the resort privileges available to you worldwide as members of the LaFontanel family."

"By the way," Howard asked before he shut the door, "Bleasdale didn't tell you what makes him really happy, did he?"

"No . . ."

"Thank God."

The door almost immediately opened after Howard left and Mr. Samson clicked in. A yellow-suited, almost handsome used car stereotype, he closed the door and sat down, comfortable in his knowledge that he was the best looking person in that room.

"My name is Dirk Samson, and I'm supposed to tell you about your fantastic vacation possibilities in the LaFontanel family of fabulous resorts. Christ, it smells like fart in here. As you well know, ownership in the LaFontanel fam. . ."

"We know, we know, ownership entitles us to two weeks' vacation per year for practically pennies in any of 127 locations worldwide." Hazel mockingly finished his sentence. "And the fart smell has to be your boss, not us."

"The pretty lady's been payin' attention!" Samson said, undressing Hazel with his eyes. She shuddered at his sledgehammer flirtatiousness. "Now, let's talk resort privileges,"

Samson continued, taking a LaFontanel catalog out of his top desk drawer. "Where do you folks typically spend your vacations?"

"We just got back from the Outer Banks a couple of weeks ago," Billy explained.

"Hmm, Outer Banks, that's in Canada. . ." Samson flipped through the slim catalog, "No, we don't have any. . .wait! We do have a place, near Manteo, North Carolina. It's called the 'Sea Foan'.

"Is that a typo?" Billy asked, "Because we drove by a dump called the 'Sea Foam' on our way out to eat one night. You remember, Hazy? It looked like it had just burned down but was still open."

Samson raised his eyebrows. "Well, none of our properties burned recently, so this must be correct, the 'Sea Foam'."

He flipped further into the catalog. "But if it's exotic locales you're after, we have three resorts in Bangladesh." Samson squinted and mutilated one of the blurbs from the catalog. "'The Ram-pour Bo-alia Resort, near the city of Raj-shah-hee, offers the savvy LaFontanel traveler commanding views of local color, especially in non-monsoon months'." He looked up at the astonished couple. "Not too shabby, huh? And it also says they got a real toilet nearby."

"Tell me, Mr. Samson," Hazel said, "does LaFontanel build in any non-third world hellholes?"

"Like where?" Samson asked, unmoved, "Tell me your dream vacation spot. I guarantee we got a resort there!"

Hazel grinned mischievously. "How about . . . Sudan?"

"Sudan," Samson muttered as he again flipped backwards through the catalog. "I know Sudan, that's in Egypt. Here we go! Whoa – check it out! You can go to Sudan every year for the next ten years and not stay in the same LaFontanel Resort twice!"

"We get the general idea here, Mr. Samson." Billy said as he and Hazel stood. "We're not interested anymore. We're leaving."

"That's what they all say." Samson closed the catalog. "Before you go, you need to sign a form verifying that I explained the resort locations with you and . . ."

"The only thing we're signing here is the title to our new car or a receipt for five grand in cash, which we would like to collect and get the hell out of here." Billy announced as he and Hazel walked briskly out of the office.

"Ok, but if you don't sign the form ya gotta go see Mr. Nimrod in office number 3 and tell him your decision." Samson said as he dug under one of his too-long, too manicured fingernails with a small pocketknife, "He's put a lot of time and effort in bringing you here today. It would only be fair. Your prize will be waiting on your way out."

Hazel knew she was going to regret this decision. "OK. Come on Billy, let's go tell the Jolly Green Freakazoid that we're not interested so we can leave."

"Be nice!" Samson yelled from the office as they walked down the stairs. "Dirtbags."

Nimrod's office – number 3 according to the plaque – was on the first floor all the way at the end of a pink hallway behind a large, heavy oak door with an antique brass doorknob and nameplate. Billy knocked on it four times.

"YAH-MERRY-CHRISTMAS" the startled mechanical voice said from inside. Hazel and Billy looked surprised at each other before they heard "COME-IN"

The door opened into a dark and gloomy office, with Nimrod's desk buried between rows and rows of brimming bookshelves and depressingly bad artwork. Christmas tree air fresheners hung everywhere.

The giant appeared to have been asleep at his desk, as his huge, light bulb-shaped milky-white head turned spookily around toward them in a slow, deliberate movement that was more robotic than alive as they walked in. His elephantine right arm was concealed under his desk.

"MRS-BENDIX-YOU-HAVE-BAD-NEWS-I-CAN-TELL" he said, holding the electronic box up to his throat with his left hand. "HAVE-A-SEAT-DON'T-BE-SHY-I-WON'T-BITE"

"Well," Hazel stammered as she and Billy eased down onto the very edges of the executive leather wing chairs that faced his desk, "Although we have enjoyed our visit today, we feel that . . ."

"YOU-KNOW-I-HAVE-PUT-MY-LIFE-INTO-LAFONTANEL" Nimrod interrupted as a solid "thump" resounded from under the desk, releasing a cloud of stink. "IT-IS-MY-ONLY-PASSION-I-WANT-TO-DIE-WHEN-SOMEONE-IS-NOT-HAPPY"

"Mr. Nimrod, that's a terrible. . ."

"ESPECIALLY-YOU-MRS-BENDIX-I-WAS *Thump! Bump!* -HOPING-WE-WOULD-SEE-A-LOT-MORE-OF-EACH-OTHER"

"It's just that LaFontanel *Wham!* doesn't fit into our plans now."

Wham! Whump! The noises got more and more boisterous until Nimrod's flailing right "arm" suddenly lurched like an angry sandworm from under the desk. It unfurled straight up, much to Hazel and Billy's shock and repulsion, curled grotesquely and slammed down on the beautiful inlaid desk with a sickening, wet slap. It then snapped and banged against his brass desk lamp, sending it to the floor with an expensive crash. Nimrod dropped his voice box on his desk, grabbed his uncontrollable arm with his left hand and wrestled it to the desktop before it did any more damage.

Billy grabbed his own wife by the arm. "Let's get the hell outta here," he sputtered as he quickly stood and pulled Hazel up, "before I throw up."

Hazel just stood there, unable to move, almost crying in horror and revulsion watching Nimrod wrestle with his own arm. Finally it settled long enough for him to snatch up the little box in a panic and press it to his throat. "YOU-FOLKS-CAN'T-LEAVE-MRS-BENDIX-YOU-CAN'T-DO-THIS-TO-ME" he "shouted" through the device as his arm whipped back and forth. "I-FOUGHT-IN-VIETNAM-FOR-UNGRATEFUL-JERKS-LIKE-YOU-   I-WAS-A-PRISONER-OF-WAR-YOU-GET-YOUR-ASSES-BACK-HERE-RIGHT-NOW"

As Billy pulled his almost catatonic wife to the door Nimrod angrily stood – a process that seemed to take a good minute – and lumbered out from behind his desk.

"DAMN-YOU-I-WAS-TORTURED *Klonk* OW" As Nimrod stood he drilled his head straight into the ceiling light fixture, knocking it wildly back and forth, casting flashing patterns through the dark room. He staggered from the blow. "I-WAS-IN-

PRISON-CAMPS"

As Nimrod stumbled Hazel tripped on the threshold strip leading out of the third office and went down on one knee. She was a wet dishrag, too weak to get up on her own.

"I-PISSED-AGENT-ORANGE"

Billy pulled her to her feet as Nimrod picked up speed, now sporting a dent in his forehead where he whacked it on the light fixture.   "I-WAS-A-P.O.W.-IN-CHINA-CAMBODIA-CHINA-CAMBODIA"

Once out in the hallway Hazel came to life. With Billy pulling her they picked up speed and jogged past framed prints of spooky, smiling mysterious men in dark suits. Everything was sinister right now. The tacky hallway seemed a mile long, and Nimrod's robot electronic voice filled the whole thing as he ducked through his door and shambled out behind them.

"CHINA-CAMBODIA-CHINA-CAMBODIA-CHINA-"

The couple got to the end of the hall and turned right past the empty welcome desk only to bump into Happy Bleasdale, who stopped them in their tracks. He held a paper and pen in his hand, and his eyes were wide and crazy, like those of a crackhead.

"You folks didn't answer my question!" he demanded. "Do you know what makes me *really* happy?"

Billy pushed past the disturbing Bleasdale then ran out the double doors to the car. Billy helped Hazel in and as he trotted around to the driver's side something dawned on him.

"Hazy, we forgot our prize. . ."

"No, we got our prize." she whimpered, "We're getting away with our lives."

Bleasdale burst out the doors and screamed at them from across the parking lot. "I've got your prize right here!"

Billy and Hazel sped away from LaFontanel and after driving in circles trying to escape the empty warehouse park made their way back to Staples Mill Road then finally to Richmond's Bellevue neighborhood almost in total silence, too sick and scared to talk.

By the time they got home it was almost 9:00 PM. After inspecting the house at his wife's insistence, Billy got a PBR from the fridge, flopped on the den couch and flipped on the TV to unwind while Hazel decided to go upstairs to bed, eager to forget the horrible events of the day.

"You coming up?" She asked before she went up the stairs.

"Give me some decompression time and I'll be there."

"Don't fall asleep. I don't wanna be up here by myself."

"Don't worry. Love you."

"Love you, too. I'm sorry I dragged you to that awful place."

Billy's exhaustion was too acute, and within minutes he drifted off – just like Hazel was afraid he would. The man could fall asleep standing up.

Once upstairs, Hazel slipped out of her clothes and walked naked into the bathroom, hoping a hot shower would calm her nerves while Billy napped. Noticing he left it a mess from the previous night's softball practice, she muttered a curse then looked around for a clothes hamper and some clean towels. Finding none, she walked back into the bedroom to her closet to get her robe. She would wake up Billy and drag him up while she was down there getting fresh towels.

Downstairs Billy was startled by someone in the den and opened his eyes. The TV was turned off, and it was very dark, and as he stared into the shadows he made out the rounded, three-dimensional proportions of a person. Thinking it was his wife, his eyes adjusted and soon he saw the figure's enormous size and huge, round head. As a hideous, twisting arm curled slowly at its side the confused shadow's mouth moved silently, like it was talking but without the box.

How the hell did Nimrod get in my house? Billy wondered, convinced he was dreaming as he watched the misshapen giant silently mouth the words "China" and "Cambodia" several times over through his non-working mouth. With a jolt Billy slammed his eyes shut to end the dream then a moment later opened them again.

Nimrod was gone. Billy only heard a car driving slowly down Avondale Avenue, its low-beam headlights dancing off the trees and picket fence that ran down the side of the back yard. "Stay outta my dreams you bastard." He muttered as he decided to go up to bed.

Upstairs as Hazel closed the closet and put on her robe she heard the bedroom door softly close and lock behind her. "You know, Billy, you left a hell of a mess with your filthy softball stuff in the bathroom. I gotta go down and get some towels and . . ."

When she turned she did not find her husband, but standing less than 10 feet in front of her was a grinning, hideous malformed giant whose head brushed their bedroom ceiling, wearing a baggy dark t-shirt, colorless high-water pants and what must have been size 30 scuffed wingtip shoes with no socks. He set Billy's unopened beer on the bed and slowly raised a white, dagger-like finger to his lips in a "Shhh" motion before he dropped the key in his pocket and pressed the black box to his throat.

"DO-NOT-SCREAM-HAZEL-I-WILL-NOT-HURT-YOU" he droned in a buzzing whisper through the box as he took a giant step closer to Hazel, who could only stand paralyzed, unable to scream if she wanted to. "I-THINK-I-AM-IN-LOVE-HAZEL-BENDIX" he hissed, cocking his massive, malformed head at an almost flirtatious angle.

"Mr. Nimrod?" She asked in a tiny, quaking voice, eyeing his curling tentacle as that rotting chemical stink drifted to her nostrils.

"WHAT-IS-IT-MY-SWEETS"

"What do you want from me?"

"I-AM-HERE-TO-MAKE-SWEET-LOVE-TO-YOU-I-AM-TWICE-THE-MAN-YOU-WILL-EVER-NEED"

Hazel backed up another step, realizing Billy's softball bat was leaning against his closet door about five feet behind her.

"YOU-LEFT-WITHOUT-YOUR-PRIZE-TODAY-I-AM-HERE-TO-DELIVER-IT"

Downstairs a snoring Billy moved on to his next dream, completely unaware of the terror his dear wife was experiencing upstairs.

Feeling alone and exposed, Hazel pulled her robe tighter and took one more step back, almost within reach of the bat. Nimrod twisted his lips up into an exaggerated parody of a kiss as a long strand of drool fell lazily all the way to the floor. "I-WANT-A-LITTLE-SUGAR-OH-HAZY-I-NEED-A-WOMAN-SO-BAD"   He shut both his eyes and bent way down toward her, making those obscene kissy-faces.

This was her opening. Hazel quick as a flash spun around, grabbed Billy's bat and in one unstoppable motion raised it over her head then swung it down with every ounce of strength she had, squarely onto the top of the giant's head with a sickening smash, crushing the entire top half of his skull and burying the bat down to his eyeballs. His head collapsed as if it were made of tempered glass and papier-mâché.

Downstairs Billy only snorted at the upstairs commotion.

Panicked and hyperventilating Hazel dropped the bat with a clatter to the floor as Nimrod stayed hunched over, not dead or even unconscious and almost unaffected by the devastating injury to his head. With a wheezing grunt, and with the top of his head crushed, the giant suddenly raised himself back up to his full height.

"OOOOOHHHHH" he moaned, his bulging eyes crossing as he tried to stay on his feet. Hazel stared in awe and revulsion at the inhumanly wounded giant as he slowly raised his left hand, put his huge thumb in his mouth and, twisting his hand downward, shoved his index finger inside his throat hole. Inflating his cheeks, he blew hard on his thumb, his face reddening, until finally his head popped back into its original shape with a disgusting *thwop* sound.

With Nimrod preoccupied with blowing his head back into shape Hazel darted around him to the bedroom door as the gnarled giant pulled his finger from his throat hole with a wet smack and shook his newly-inflated skull, as if he were making sure everything worked.

"HAZY-WHERE-ARE-YOU-GOING-YOU-LITTLE-MINX" he sneered drunkenly as he suddenly sat clumsily on their bed, folding that huge, ungainly body into a sitting position and crossing his long, spindly legs. "YOU-LOOKING-FOR-THIS" he asked as he held the bedroom door key up in the pincers at the end of his tentacle-arm as Hazel in blind panic yanked helplessly on the locked door.

"I-CAN-DO-A-TRICK-WATCH" he stuck out his gnarled tongue and lay the key on it with his good hand. Hazel looked over her shoulder in disgust as he swallowed the key then retrieved it as it emerged from his throat hole. "TA-DAAA".

Nimrod put the key back in his pocket, laid his voice box on the bed, and with much difficulty picked up and opened Billy's beer. Never taking his eyes off Hazel, he took a long drink and it all promptly sprayed out of his hole down the front of his filthy shirt. "YOU-ARE-PLAYING-HARD-TO-GET-YOU-HOT-TAMALE" he hissed as he pulled a pack of Marlboros from his pocket, winked and inserted one into the beer-soaked opening. He produced a small box of wooden matches from another pocket and lit the cigarette, drawing a long, nauseating inhale before exhaling the smoke through the gaping cavity.

As Nimrod put the cigarette back in Hazel noticed he seemed to "zone out" for a moment, as if he was having a seizure, possibly from the blow to the head. With the intruder momentarily out of contention she suddenly turned, beat her fists on the old wooden door and screamed "BILLY!" as loud as she could.

Whether it was the cheesy lawyer commercial on TV at that moment which featured the whine of an ambulance siren or his wife's scream that woke Billy, he literally leapt from the couch and bounded up the stairs as Hazel's pounding on the locked bedroom door reached a fevered pitch. She cut loose yet another wrenching "BILLY!"

In a blind fury, Billy dove for the doorknob. Finding it locked he unsuccessfully threw his shoulder into it but it refused to budge. He tried again, with no luck. Damn that 1930s solid wood construction! As he was about to try a third time he heard Hazel whisper softly to him from inside. He stopped and with his chest about to explode put his ear up to the door.

"Billy," the terrified voice said quietly from the other side, "Please get me the hell out of here."

"HAZEL-HAZEL-HAZEL" a now horrified Billy heard from inside the room with her, "DUMP-THAT-CHUMP-YOU-COULD-HAVE-A-REAL-MAN-LIKE-ME"

Smelling Nimrod's body odor and cigarette smoke gave Billy a thousand ideas but only one good one. "I'll be right back honey," he whispered as he tore back down the stairs, around the corner down to his basement workshop. He figured that Nimrod's crush on his wife would buy him a few precious minutes.

In the basement Billy tore everything apart until he found a wooden box containing about six miscellaneous skeleton keys left by the previous owner. Cramming them into his pants pocket he scavenged furiously until he found a bag of balloons that he hid for

Hazel's 34th birthday party.

He ripped open the balloon bag, removed one and stretched it over the narrow end of a plastic funnel. He turned his lawnmower gas can upside down and filled the balloon with gasoline, making a poor man's molotov cocktail.

Once the balloon contained about a half-pint of gas Billy tied it and ran back up to the second floor, the six old keys jingling in his pocket. About halfway up to the bedroom he slowed and listened carefully, hearing Nimrod still talking about a kiss. He tiptoed to the door, knelt and laid down the balloon while he quietly fished the keys out of his pocket.

"HAZY-THAT-WASN'T-NICE-HOW-YOU-CRUSHED-MY-HEAD" Nimrod said angrily, losing patience with Hazel because she wouldn't respond to his advances. "GET-OVER-HERE-AND-KISS-MY-BOOBOO"

Still against the bedroom door, Hazel could hear the gentle rustle of her husband on the other side, gently inserting one of the old keys in the door. She heard it jiggle unsuccessfully, then pull out. Then he gently inserted another one, repeating the procedure.

After the third unsuccessful try Billy got agitated as he watched his gas balloon start to sweat – the first sign that the rubber was deteriorating and would soon burst. Perspiration beads popped up on his forehead and upper lip as he removed the third key and quickly inserted the fourth, his hand starting to shake with panic. He cursed as he jiggled the fourth key, then removed it. He only had two keys left, and if neither one worked he was going to have a huge problem.

"I-HAVE-A-BOO-BOO-RIGHT-HERE-THAT-NEEDS-A-KISS"

Nimrod pouted, pointing to the top of his stringy-haired, re-inflated head. Seeing Hazel was ignoring him he moaned, uncrossed his legs and started the long, cumbersome process of standing up. Hazel turned her head slightly from the door to see the horrific giant reach his full standing height, the lit cigarette sticking out from his throat like a tiny white erection.

He took a long draw and blew a perfect smoke ring through the hole before pressing the box to his throat. "I-HAVE-TIRED-OF-YOUR-TEASING-ME" he announced through the box before he unzipped his pants. "TIME-FOR-NIMROD-TO-GET-HIS-PAYMENT-IN-PERPETUITY"

Billy turned the fifth key and the latch slowly slipped back into the striker, unlocking the door, much to his relief but with a renewed sense of even stronger panic. With the door now unlocked, he gently picked up the ever-softening balloon in his left hand, slowly turning the doorknob with his right.

Inside, Hazel, to her great relief, saw the knob turning. Suddenly sensing that Billy was putting a stop to this nightmare, she briefly turned to face the dreadful giant. He loomed less than four feet from her, his giant eyebrows wagging lustfully, his good hand buried in his open zipper, his stench making her eyes water. It was like standing in front of a horny decomposing dinosaur.

"Go to hell, Nimrod."

"TSK-TSK-HAZY-I-HAVE-A-BETTER-USE-FOR-THAT-POTTY-MOUTH"

With the hollow words "potty mouth" the door suddenly opened. Billy grabbed his wife by the top of her head and with a burst of strength shoved her straight down out of the way. Hazel ducked down, squeezing through the open doorway past her husband who stood holding his sweating gas bomb. Nimrod never flinched at the activity, blowing another perfectly-formed smoke ring through his trach hole, a sick grin lingering on his loathsome face.

With Hazel out of the way, Billy went into his best company softball pitcher windup and with a prayer threw the almost-degraded balloon at the malformed monster, striking him directly on the left collarbone.

The balloon burst in a gassy flammable splash upon impact, and Nimrod's cigarette erupted his huge milky head in a bursting bluish-white ball of hot roaring flame that seemed to fill the entire room. He jerked his hand out of his pants, and through the fire Billy briefly saw his huge yawning mouth open wide in a desperate, silent scream.

Hazel and Billy tore down the stairs and straight through the foyer. Finding the front door locked, Billy fumbled through his pockets for his keys. "Hurry Billy hurry!" Hazel pleaded as Billy searched his pockets. Searches done in a panic always went slower.

Suddenly they heard a huge, irregular tromping noise as the blazing giant started down the old oak staircase after them. His crazy tentacle-arm banged against the walls and banisters wildly as he clumped desperately toward them, his entire upper body engulfed in crackling white-hot flame. Hazel glanced up the stairs long enough to see only his huge feet and legs clumsily descending the stairs just as Billy found his keys, inserted first the wrong one, then the correct one in the deadbolt. He turned the key, threw open the door, and both of them ran straight out across the yard onto the Laburnum Avenue median, where they stopped and looked back at their house through the open front door.

They saw a huge flaming object moving erratically inside their home. First it seemed to stop, then move again, then stop, as if it couldn't find its way out. They watched in horror and confusion as suddenly a short, heavyset man, with his head and upper body ablaze screamed in muffled agony as he struggled out of the house onto the lawn. Staggering halfway across the yard, he dropped to his knees, then collapsed face-down.

After the intruder in the yard burned himself out, and didn't move for several minutes, Hazel and Billy walked over hand-in-hand and looked down at the charred and smoldering body of the man who had first called Hazel; the same man who met and welcomed them at the resort and whom they accused of listening in through the door. It was the lifeless body of Howard DeRoach, or Nimrod, or whatever physical metamorphosis he preferred, it really no longer mattered, because he was now quite dead.

Around the corner two doors down inside a lone sedan a black man with gelled-back hair and a swarthy white man with several gold chains around his neck watched the activity in the yard from the front seat.

"DeRoach struck out." The black man said. "I told him not to come on so strong."

The white guy sighed. "Looks like it's your turn, soul man."

"Great!" The black man opened his car door, stood and yelled to the Bendix's. "Hey! Do you folks know what makes me *really* happy?"

Sig's Place

Phil Budahn

Sig Ismonde spent a long time looking for the perfect spot for Le Chat Noire. Word on the street said Sig had irregularities in his financing -- certain technicalities involving the original ownership of his working capital and the manner of its transfer to his accounts -- that disinclined him from rushing the grand opening of his club.

Sig always put down the delay to "finding a place where the right kind of angels sing." There's a dozen ways to explain that line, any one of which could be right on target, but knowing Sig it's likely all possible answers combined won't add up to a famished half-truth.

And when he finally settled on the back end of a long-closed dressmakers near the corner of Grace and 5th, accessible only by an alley where shadows clung to the sweaty brick walls and the same puddles were there during droughts and blizzards, the wiseguys said Sig had reasons of his own for finding a hole he could throw a bundle into.

Weren't we surprised when the place started packing them in.

Of course, it didn't hurt for the customers to lay eyes on Connie the moment they stepped in the door. Connie reminded the city's old-timers of other reasons to tremble, what with legs that started at the ground and didn't know when to quit, and eyes so cool you couldn't stop thinking about ways to break through the ice. That woman gave heart-ache a good name.

Sleepy jazz uncoiled through the cigarette smoke like a cat stretching its legs; the shadows were so thick some of Le Chat Noire's best customers swore they never laid eyes on VanDaMirr, the bartender, whose twisted nose and glaring eyes were enough to sober the rowdiest character. Even under those atmospherics, with Connie to serve them, it's easy to understand the lack of interest in what was hiding in the dark. That was part of the joint's appeal, and like I said, having Connie didn't hurt.

Only a couple duffers remember seeing a guy wander in one night with a cheap oversized suitcase that had *Thomas Cudlup and Sparky* printed on the sides. The stranger had a few words with Sig, so Sig listened without looking from his ashtray, nodded, then the fellow walked out, almost clearing three tables of linen, glasses and customers with his luggage. The next evening the suitcase sat on a chair by the brick wall near the jazz combo, and when the boys took a break after their first set, from around the corner that led to Sig's office came that stranger with an odd-looking package in his arms.

The guy parked himself on a barstool, the package began to move, and by the time that little bundle quit squirming, every eye in the place was watching him. He was holding a little man, a ventriloquist's dummy. Its hair was strawy orange, the eyes, nose and mouth a bit exaggerated, but except for that, the dummy was a pretty good replica of the stranger.

"We're Thomas Cudlup and Sparky," the guy said.

The dummy looked at the guy. Slowly, it rotated its head to the audience and said, "I'm Thomas Cudlup."

And the guy said, "I'm Sparky."

The routine was a twenty-minute riff of that gag: Thomas Cudlup, the dummy, did the talking, and the guy, Sparky, had the punch lines. Sparky sat there with blank, glassy eyes, and when he spoke, his voice had a strained, unnatural tone. After a while, fingers in the audience started pointing and the whisper spread that if you watched Thomas Cudlup's lips, you'd see them moving a little whenever Sparky said something. By the end of the show, Thomas Cudlup drank a glass of water while Sparky hummed a tune and everyone was so confused it seemed a remarkable accomplishment.

That performance made a regular of Sparky -- guess he was one of Sig's "right sort of angels." Hard to explain now, but Sparky helped set the tone in Le Chat Noire as much as slow jazz, the fog banks of cigarette smoke, Connie's cool eyes or VanDaMirr's broken nose. Sig spent the better part of that first week walking around with an odd expression that the drummer ascribed to hemorrhoids while the trumpet player said it was the closest the man got to happy. Customers were heard to ask VanDaMirr twice for their drinks when Sparky was on, and Connie reputedly let a client or two slip into the club without her attentions.

Sparky was an ordinary guy drifting somewhere between his late 30s and mid 40s, a bit thinner than average, whose stark black hair made the top of his head disappear sometimes into the darkness of the club. He moved as though his body, from the waist to the neck, was one piece owing to his habit of keeping his left hand in the pocket of his sports coat except when he was working with Thomas Cudlup. Connie said he had a tarnished, debonair look.

Anyone could glance at him and tell he was new to the city: his eyes rested on twin half-moon bruises at the top of his cheeks, and even during his act, he shuffled around like a guy eight hours short of a good night's sleep. *Beaten* isn't a bad description for old Sparky. Unlike the rest of the dreamers, dopes and malcontents who wander into downtown and can't find a reason to leave, Sparky didn't lash out at the injustices upon which every brick rested nor did he search for a wise man to tell him what to do or a mother to take care of him.

"He took to the place like he was born here," Sig said in a way that made VanDaMirr wonder whether his boss was disappointed or proud or both.

VanDaMirr was the first to notice that Sparky didn't have fingerprints. Not that it took a psychic or a gumshoe to come up with that revelation. What's VanDaMirr got to do with his spare time except look at glasses that have been in people's hands?

When he mentioned it to Connie, she gave him a Connie-look, which was enough to leave most men with a dopey smile for a couple days. But VanDaMirr didn't do smiles.

Before the end of the week, Sparky had his routine set in concrete. Come 5:45 each evening, we'd hear his footsteps thumping up the alley. Even the bus boys remarked on Sparky's stride. Heavier than you'd expect, and slow enough to make you wonder if Sparky was carrying more of a load than he let on to. As if Thomas Cudlup wasn't your average package of wood splints, cloth, papier-mâché, and paint.

Connie would be at her counter by the front door, and as

Sparky passed, there'd be this muffled thin whistle, then a muffled voice saying, "Hiya, doll," like Thomas Cudlup was talking from inside the suitcase. Even the mugs who counted their major life events in broken knuckles and lost teeth would get a silly ain't-that-cute grin.

A couple more steps by Sparky and those grins dissolved into something nervy, squirmy. 'Cause, loud enough to hear in the kitchen, there'd be this knocking, RAP-rap-rap-RAP-RAP, like the beginning of the old "shave and a haircut" shtick, and everyone could see both of Sparky's hands and the only way that tapping could be made was by something hard and tiny -- say, a ventriloquist's dummy's tiny fists -- knocking on the inside of a Samsonite case.

At precisely, 6 p.m., Sparky would walk up the little hallway from the back, settle on his stool and say, "We're Thomas Cudlup and Sparky."

Like I said, the dummy's head would rotate slowly, like he's studying the audience, then say, "I'm Thomas Cudlup."

And the guy would say, "I'm Sparky."

As many times as folks heard it, it still cracked them up.

The patter was mostly fresh, although you couldn't begrudge a stand-up for recycling his best material from time to time. But Sparky didn't go for that, not in any wholesale way, and after a while, you'd hear some of the regulars say that that'd explain the way Sparky stayed in the back between shows, why he didn't mingle with the staff or the customers, why you never saw him around town. No one ever saw him around town. He was working on his act.

Of course, there was talk. In place like Sig's there's always talk. The smart ones were careful what they said around the big guy or VanDaMirr. And Connie. Though in Connie's case, it wasn't the fear of getting your head thumped that encouraged politeness.

Long about a month after Sparky's arrival, Sig's place was stretching its legs and starting to swagger. The college kids and expense-account guys were showing up, thanks to a couple brightly polished adjectives in the *Times-Dispatch*.

Sig shrugged whenever one of the boys in pin-stripes thought Sig needed advice on marketing plans and business projections. Things were going good, and Sig was never one to draw another card when he knew he had a winning hand. Besides, the boys from the old days were always welcome.

Well, perhaps, not everybody. VanDaMirr had an old business associate from his time working bars in Norfolk that catered to the fleet. Timmy Tabasco was how we knew him. He was broad in the waist and narrow around the hat band, if you get the drift, but that only made Timmy T- more likely to insist on getting whatever respect wasn't coming his way naturally.

The night Timmy saw Sparky and Thomas Cudlup walk to that stool for the first time, you'd think the Queen of England had appeared in the all-together. Timmy couldn't take his eyes off them.

VanDaMirr asked Timmy if he'd seen the pair before, and Timmy signaled for a refill, said, "Yep, but he was working solo back then," and, so far as the cops could later piece together, never spoke to anyone else in the place. Never, in fact, spoke to anyone else, period.

Next morning a garbage crew found Timmy in an alley, bled to death. Which seemed like a slow exit for a mug who could have cleared out Sig's joint any night he felt feisty. But the coroner said Timmy had gotten it when and where he least expected, and some of the boys in blue said the geniuses in the lab coats were too quick to rule out the possibility of an accident. A freaky, inexplicable and one-of-a-kind accident. Sure. But freaky made more sense than the fantasy that someone would decide to take out Timmy Tabasco by driving a screwdriver into an artery.

If Sig ever said a word about Timmy's passing it was in his sleep and, even then, only when he was sleeping alone. Some of the fellas speculated as to how there might be a connection between the deep pockets that kept Sig's place open during the early tough days and Timmy's fatal encounter with a common household implement. Timmy wasn't on Sig's Christmas card list, but the death took something out of the big guy, or maybe it dropped something on him. Connie, when she heard that line of reasoning, said quietly that both things had happened to Sig at the same time.

A couple months after Timmy's demise, the next shoe fell. Big time. And Sig and VanDaMirr found themselves alone, after hours, in the back room where Sig let the staff park their stuff and take a breather from time to time. Every lipstick tube, perfume bottle, eye-liner stick and powder puff that VanDaMirr put into a cardboard box was a little burial. You can talk about gals like Connie being a dime a dozen, but try finding the other eleven.

"It was toward the end of his first week," Sig said. "I came back here looking for Connie when Sparky was on. Didn't find her, but I couldn't help but notice his bag. One whole side was down, and you couldn't guess what was inside."

"A little girl dummy setting a table."

"Tools." Sig went on like he hadn't heard VanDaMirr, which was probably the case. "Wires. Electrical parts. Transformers, microchips, oscilloscopes. Enough to stock your own repair shop."

"Don't go there," VanDaMirr snapped. "Anyone can own a screwdriver. Don't prove nothing." He sniffed a pad of rouge, fought the urge to dab it on his fingers. "You ever really notice Thomas Cudlup's skin? It's --"

"It's what?"

"It's more real than Sparky's, more real than anyone else in the joint. Like that little dummy was the only genuine article here."

"Stranger things have happened."

Sig rose, stretched and stepped to his desk. VanDaMirr had to flatten himself against a shelf of glasses and silverware for the boss to pass. Ever since Sig gave up his office to Sparky and moved into the supply room, there'd barely been space to turn around.

While Sig flipped through the papers on his desk, VanDaMirr packed the last of Connie's things. He wanted to get out of there before Sig got sloppy and started talking about Connie. Or Timmy. Some things only an idiot wants to know.

Funny, but a cheap packet of bobby pins hit him the hardest. Women put them into their hair to look nice; they aren't supposed to be seen by anyone else, and that made the little bundle of twisted, lacquered wires the most intimate contact he would ever have with Connie.

He looked at Sig. "Do you think she made it out of here?"

"She changed addresses."

Sig must have noticed a drop in the temperature of the little room -- for all his bluster and rough edges, he was rarely wrong about a drink needing refreshing or a hand of cards that should be folded; he wheeled on VanDaMirr like he just realized the man was there.

"Did you ever get a good look at Sparky's left hand, the one that was always in his pocket?"

"You mean, the one with the fingers?"

Sig stretched an arm to the door frame; he could have been steadying the building. By this point, he had to realize his bartender didn't know the score.

"I saw Sparky behind the bar one night before we opened," Sig said. "He had a glass of water in one hand and he slipped on something back there -- a napkin on the floor, a wet tile, I don't know. Out went the hand from his pocket to keep from landing on his puss. You know what was on it?"

"Six fingers?" VanDaMirr said. "Seven, eight?"

"There was this little metal band. First I thought he was wearing brass-knuckles. Then I saw these little lights embedded in the metal -- orange, red, white. They were blinking. And some tiny dials and stuff."

"Some sort of control. Right?"

When Sig nodded, VanDaMirr slapped his leg and said, "I knew it. I'd watch that dummy, and sometimes Thomas Cudlup would move his head and blink his eyes when Sparky wasn't touching him. I knew he had to have some sort of wireless controls."

"Something like that." Sig jerked his head toward the door. "Come here for a minute."

The box with Connie's things jingled like a baby's toybox as VanDaMirr set it on a chair and followed his boss into the hallway. Instead of turning right toward the club, Sig went left toward his old office that Sparky now used. It had been a while since VanDaMirr had stood this close to Sig, and he was startled to remember how broad in the shoulders he was. You don't carve out a niche in the city unless you are willing to put some muscle behind it.

Suddenly, VanDaMirr was afraid. He didn't want to go any further. Sig had secrets he'd been carrying a long time, and anyone who shared the load also shared the risks. Even in a dump like this, it was possible to slide lower. Maybe that's what Connie had done.

"She told me a story once." VanDaMirr started talking before he entirely knew why this memory was important now, unless he sensed he was about to step further into Sig's world, and he wanted to come clean about Connie because there wouldn't be a chance to balance the books later. "She followed Sparky from the club one night. She didn't say why and I didn't ask. They ended up heading toward the river."

"Did he have the dummy with him?"

"Yeah."

Sig turned partially toward VanDaMirr. The boss stood in the darkness like something carved of stone that had always been there and would always be there, that wouldn't let the city make another mark on him.

VanDaMirr continued, "Sparky went past a bunch of abandoned warehouses behind Tobacco Row. Then he went through the side door of one old wreck -- some sort of boarded-up, abandoned store. Connie says she waited a half hour or so."

While Sig gave him a few moments to collect his thoughts, VanDaMirr realized where his tale was heading, and he had a pretty good idea the boss wouldn't like the end of the story. Sig turned toward him. In the shadows of the hallway, it was like Sig had no face.

"Go on," Sig prodded.

VanDaMirr swallowed hard. "So she went inside, too. It was storage for the sort of electronic stuff you were talking about. Gadgets and wires and fancy-doodle gizmos."

"And then?"

"The kid got weepy. She never finished."

"When did this happen?"

VanDaMirr clenched his teeth and braced his legs. He never should have opened his trap. But Sig deserved the straight-at-you truth, and if VanDaMirr had to take a jab or two, it wouldn't be the first time.

"Her last night here."

If it wasn't for the intense breaths working their way through Sig's nostrils, VanDaMirr might have thought his boss had turned into a statue. For long seconds, they stood there, Sig breathing deep and hard, and when he turned without a word and walked down the hallway, VanDaMirr followed. The bartender wondered if his boss could hear the thunder of his heart beats.

"I figured," VanDaMirr said, "what with those blinking lights you saw on Sparky's hand, there must be a connection. What do you say?"

Sig spun the knob of his old office, pushed the door open and stood aside. The light inside wasn't much better than the hallway. VanDaMirr wondered how a large cat had gotten into the room. Then he saw Sparky slumped in the corner on a stool, his eyes wide and his mouth hanging open, his chin on his chest. And Thomas Cudlup standing between his knees, screwdriver in hand, as he removed a silver panel from the ventriloquist's chest.

Hunting Joey Banks

Meriah L. Crawford

I was hunched in the corner of a small, rickety tree house overlooking a backyard in Church Hill near midnight, struggling madly not to move. I had the mother of all leg cramps, and it took everything I had not to holler with pain and try to massage it out. Since becoming a vampire two years ago, I'd become stronger in almost every way--but when I go too long without a red meal, the pains kick in with a vengeance. If I'd been home, I'd have been rocking back and forth, cursing loudly, but any movement would alert the four men talking in the hedges below that I was there, and my investigation would be over before it really even started. Worse, my client would almost certainly end up dead, and while that might not exactly be a tragedy, it would definitely be awkward.

I longed to call my friend Peri, who was a truly gifted healing witch. She could have at least taken the edge off my pain, even over the phone, but there was no way to do it quietly. I'd already discovered that the tree house made loud creaking noises if I did so much as turn my head too suddenly. I just hoped it wouldn't collapse under me before the meeting ended.

My video camera was filming everything that went on below me, and I was pretty sure I'd planted the microphone in the right spot. Because my hearing was extra-sensitive now, I could hear most of their words even without my gear.

I'm pretty open-minded, especially nowadays—a vamp can't really be too judgemental, after all—but these bastards, they were planning a hunt. Not deer or elk or bear, which would be bad enough to my mind, but a man. Of course, I hunted men, too—and the occasional woman, for variety—but I almost never killed them. It was unnecessary, and just plain wasteful. You can't take blood from a corpse. And animals? Even if their blood was enough to sustain me—and for some reason, it wasn't—I still wouldn't hunt them. Their fear during the chase always made me sad—made me want to run and rescue them. I'd felt like that since I was a little kid, rescuing cats from the street or lifting baby birds back into their nests.

It wasn't the first time, but I felt like a bad vampire for not being blood-thirsty enough, vicious enough. All I had to do was think about my client and the four guys below me, and that worry passed. Before this case was over, there would be blood enough for any vampire.

Most of what the men were saying to each other was the usual male bullshit.

"I'm gonna kill that bastard."

"Yeah, not if I get to him first."

"Gonna make that bastard suffer. Make him wish he never set foot in this state."

"He was born here, dipshit."

"Yeah, whatever."

Followed by the obligatory discussion about guns:

"Man, my M-4 is gonna leave a hole in him the size of a barn."

"No way, my AR-180..." Blah, blah, blah.

I held my position, silently cursing them all. They couldn't have done this on the phone or in an e-mail? Somewhere I could sit up straight, relaxed, listening or watching in relative comfort? The cloak and dagger stuff was, I expected, more for show or for fun than for any practical reasons. But it meant I'd gone longer than I liked without a good meal. Why couldn't they invent a blood-based trail mix or energy bar?

The men moved on to a debate about the merits of Glocks versus Sigs. The skinny guy made a pitch for Berettas, which the others responded to with contempt.

I wasn't that religious about guns myself, but like a lot of women, I'd found that Glocks didn't fit my hands well. My handguns are all Sigs. In fact, one of them was digging into my right side at that moment, balancing out the pain in my left leg a little too well. I hate doing surveillance. Hate it.

Finally the tall, bulky one cleared his throat and they all fell silent. He said, "You guys talk too damn much. First, no M-4s or other fancy bullshit. We all take shotguns. We use Remington buck, like every other hunter does. We load with gloves so there are no prints on the shells. And we keep our mouths closed. No grandstanding. The hunt isn't for fun. It's to send a message. Nobody messes with the Senator, or his grandkids. This sonofabitch *pays*."

After nodding and grumbling their understanding, the men agreed on a time and place to meet: the next day, 6 a.m., at the logging road off 33. That didn't help me a lot. Route 33 was a long, winding two-lane highway, and the logging road they referred to could be almost anywhere. I was thinking I'd have to get my car and watch one of their houses all night, when one of the other two, who smelled oddly like honey, told the skinny guy he'd pick him up at five. We were at Honey's house, so all I'd have to do was arrive early enough to follow him.

"Don't make me wait this time, dumbass," skinny guy said, as they walked off toward their cars.

Finally, I heard the last car drive away from the house and Honey's front door slam. I grabbed my phone and tapped Peri's name as the wooden platform under me sent a sharp warning sound into the night air. When Peri answered, all I had to do was say "Leg, leg," and I heard her begin to murmur words in Latin. Almost instantly, I felt the tickle of magic energy creep down my leg and begin untying the knots in my muscle. When she was done, all that was left was a dull ache that would fade in an hour or two. Amazing.

After promising Peri my undying gratitude, with chocolate sauce and a cherry on top, I climbed down and slid through the bushes at the side of the yard toward my car. The men never said his name. They called him the prey, the quarry, the animal—but I knew his name. He was my client: Josiah Bankston. Naturally, his buddies called him Joey Banks, but he'd told me, in what was either a touching moment of honesty or a really good act, that he hated the nickname, said it made him sound like a two-bit Hollywood hoodlum. Josiah just didn't fit, though, and everyone but his momma knew it.

Joe, as we'd agreed I would call him, was a target because he'd just gotten out of prison. When I heard what he'd been in for, I almost got up and walked out, but there was a look on his face that made me sit and hear him out. When he told me he was innocent, I lifted my left eyebrow, and he frowned. "I will take a polygraph. I will swear on the graves of every last one of my ancestors. Hell, I will even submit to a witch's scan. I. Did. Not. Do it."

It was the offer to accept a witch's scan that convinced me to give him a chance. A scan left no secrets. Few people were innocent enough or stupid enough to expose themselves that way. It was also a felony, either to perform one or to willingly have one done on yourself, thanks to some ferocious lobbying by the religious right. Maybe he thought I wouldn't go there, wouldn't take the risk. But I would. And I did. Not the whole risk, mind you. Just enough that another witch friend could do a quick, targeted scan from a distance and tell me for sure that he hadn't molested his kids, or anyone else's. Never had, never would.

When I talked to her later she told me, "People who do that sort of thing have a taste...a smell. When you look inside their minds, it's like there's something nasty in the corner, slowly rotting, rippling with maggots. This guy, I can tell he's no boy scout, but he doesn't have that." She looked so relieved; for the first time I got a sense of why most witches had refused to scan criminals, even before it was illegal.

The clean scan plus the sad state of my bank account made me take the case. The retainer was huge. The check cleared. And all I had to do was prove he was innocent. A tough case for most PIs, but with my powers of persuasion—made up of implied threats and manipulation more than violence, for the most part—I thought it would be fairly straightforward. It was a good case.

Or it was until Joey got kidnapped. In fairness to me, it happened the same day he hired me. I'd barely gotten started on the case--and after all, I was supposed to be investigating the past, not acting as his bodyguard. Considering the fact that the two goons who'd been guarding him ended up dead, that was probably just as well. But, yeah, it was embarrassing anyway. And it was just luck that I'd been able to pull the case together quickly and get a lead on the guys who'd taken Joe.

The next morning, I arrived at Honey's house while it was still dark. I got there at a little past 3:30--leaving plenty of time in case he decided to head out early for a stop at Starbucks, say. But Honey didn't seem to have any early-morning plans. The lights in his mustard-yellow two-story house went on at 4:10, and the front door opened almost 20 minutes later. Following him in town was a breeze. There were enough cars that it wasn't obvious I was trailing him, but not so many I risked losing him at a light.

After about 25 minutes, Honey stopped at a townhouse in a small development off Parham Road, near the mall, and picked up the other guy. From there, they drove north then northwest out of town, keeping to the local roads. What little traffic there was at that hour gradually thinned out by the time we reached Montpelier, and I dropped farther and farther back, just barely keeping them in sight. They maintained a constant speed without stopping until we arrived at a logging road, just before reaching a little town called Mineral. The road was around a sharp bend, and there was so much tall grass and brush at the entrance that I might have missed it if I hadn't seen them turn. I kept driving after they pulled in, finding what looked like a little-used driveway nearby where I parked my car and followed on foot.

I thought I might be in for a long run, but they didn't go far. Apparently they weren't planning a very long hunt--or at least not a challenging one. As I reached a broad oak just a few feet from them, I saw the big guy pop his trunk and reach in. He hauled out a disheveled but generally healthy-looking Josiah Bankston, with his hands cuffed in front of him and his ankles duct taped together. More duct tape covered his mouth. The look on Joe's face showed a mix of fury and fear. It made me feel sorry for him, and at the same time...hungry. He smelled like prey. It smelled very, very good.

I did my best to ignore it. I'd had a small snack the night before--enough to take the edge off without dulling my senses. It was a difficult balance, always, and this time I'd obviously taken too little. By the time I realized I'd been hyper-focused on Joe's soft, warm neck, I'd already missed part of the conversation. But what followed was impossible to miss. Big man ripped the duct tape from Joe's face, causing him to yelp. A few drops of blood glistened on his upper lip in the early light, like dew. The drops swelled as the wounds oozed, like sweet, ripe berries growing on a vine... I shook my head sharply, struggling to focus.

"--innocent!" Joe was shouting. "I didn't do it. I would never hurt those kids. They mean the world to me."

Yeah, except at least one of the three wasn't even his, as he'd explained when we first met. His wife apparently had a short attention span. Not that I could blame her after talking to him for a couple hours.

"Aw, ain't that sweet?" the skinny guy said. "Banks here molested his kids because he loved them so much." His back was to me so I couldn't see his face, but the kick that he aimed at the side of Joe's knee made it clear how he felt. Joe collapsed when the kick landed, howling in pain. The prey was injured and afraid now.

Fear always gave the blood a spicy taste. Slightly bitter. So nice.

Joe started up his protestations of innocence again as he lurched to his feet, ripping the tape around his ankles apart, but the big guy shouted him down. "Enough! You did it; we know you did it. Your wife, rest her soul, made that very, very clear to the Senator before she took her life. Anything you got to say is bullshit." He emphasized the point by racking the slide on his shotgun. The others, holding their guns with varying degrees of comfort, readied themselves.

The information about Joe's wife and father-in-law was interesting, but I was out of time. I had a job to do. Almost before I'd decided who to take first, I was out from behind the tree and moving. The skinny guy was closest. I grabbed his chin in one hand and the back of his head in another and twisted, hard. When I heard and felt that satisfying crunch, I released him and moved toward Honey. I took him the same way, and before the first guy had even hit the ground I was onto the third guy. He'd seen movement, heard something, and started to turn by then. But not anywhere near quickly enough.

My heart was roaring in my chest by then, that freaky supercharged vamp adrenaline flooding my body. It was a glorious feeling—like I was invincible.

I grabbed the throat of the third man and ripped it out, blood spouting from the gigantic, jagged wound. And then the big man. He'd actually gotten his shotgun up and started aiming it in my direction. Excellent.

He fired as I dove to the ground, rolled, and kicked at his knee. As he collapsed, I could feel the buckshot tear into my right thigh, but it was meaningless. The wound was like sunlight reflecting off a lake—harsh, pretty, sparkling, but ultimately harmless. I laughed. It almost felt good.

Big man knew this wasn't just a fight—it was *the* fight. Possibly the last fight he would ever have. He lurched to his feet, swinging the stock of the shotgun at my head, just missing me as I dodged the blow, moving faster than his eyes could even track. I grabbed the shotgun and wrenched it from his grip, tossing it behind me into the woods. I laughed at the look of shock on his face, and he turned and began to run.

I wanted so badly to chase him—to let him stay just a step ahead, to feel his terror, his desperation, before taking him and drinking my fill. But I had other priorities.

I sprang toward him, arcing into the air, landing hard on his shoulders, knocking him forward. I yanked hard on his jaw, and felt his neck snap, followed by the impact of both of us hitting the ground, his body still twitching under me.

And Joe still stood there, gaping, dizzy, and in pain.

When I got up and turned my attention on him, he took a step back, nearly collapsing from the pain in his knee. I took a moment to compose myself and try to ease the predatory snarl off my face, then asked if he was OK.

"Uhhhh, yeah. I'm good. You?"

"Fine. Need some help?"

He looked around and took it all in, finally starting to relax. He smiled stiffly. "I think you've done enough for one day. You saved my life."

I shrugged, stepped up to him, and snapped his handcuffs apart, smirking at his flinch. "Car's that way," I said, pointing in what I hoped was the right direction. I love the woods, but I've always had a terrible sense of direction. Not a great quality in someone who spends a lot of time wandering around in strange places.

Joey grabbed one of the shotguns, made sure the safety was on, and used it like a cane. A shame—it had a gorgeous wooden stock that was going to get banged up quickly.

I wiped prints from everything else I'd touched and followed him. When he heard me behind him, he immediately started talking, the way people do when they've just come through something scary and they're so damn glad to be alive. He told me about how he'd been taken, how they'd beaten him up, how he'd spent the whole night in the trunk of the car and nearly had to piss himself before they let him out that morning, just before they drove him out to the logging road.

As I listened to him talk, I focused on movements and sounds in the trees. My senses were at their most sensitive just after a good fight. I could hyper focus on the pileated woodpecker a hundred feet up in the trees, or the well-camouflaged eastern fence lizard sunning on a rock in a clearing off to the right. And I wanted to. I tried to make myself think only of the birds and snakes and chipmunks making their way through the woods, but I was so, so hungry. I muttered "Not prey, not prey, not prey" under my breath, like a mantra. But, like a fool, Joey Banks kept right on talking.

He couldn't believe they really thought he'd molest those kids. He couldn't understand why the courts wouldn't grant him some kind of visitation. He couldn't believe that bitch had thought she'd get away with telling those lies about him.

And the way she always nagged at him about driving the kids around after he'd had a few - like he couldn't handle a car after a couple of beers. And the way she complained about his being too rough with his two sons, as if a little rough-housing and name calling to toughen them up was gonna do them any harm.

And the look on her face when he showed her the suicide note he'd typed up for her. The way she begged him not to do it. The way he acted like he was reconsidering, and the pathetic look of hope on her face when he pretended to change his mind.

That one - it was so funny he stopped in his tracks, roaring with laughter.

And what was really funny is how he never even considered for a moment that he'd just confessed to murdering a woman who was trying to protect her children while a hungry vampire was walking behind him through a deserted section of forest. And he was injured prey.

I stepped forward, grabbed his neck, tipped him backwards against my chest, and bit down on the left side of his neck. He fought of course, fought hard, but I'm even stronger when I'm angry - and I was very, very angry. I drank and drank, savoring the blood: dark, dangerous, powerful. And I would have it all.

The prey kicked at me, dug his heels into the dirt, arched his back, clawed at me with his hands. And still his blood flowed. He managed one decent punch at my right cheek before I twisted his arm sharply, making bones snap. He tried to cry out for help, but I clamped my hand tighter around his neck, and before long his resistance began to weaken. His heart struggled; the flow began to ease. A few seconds more, and his legs collapsed. We sank to the ground together, and soon I sucked the last of his blood from the wound on his neck.

Finally, I released him and sat back, lolling against a tree. I was so full. Sated. My body flush with endorphins, my very cells singing with joy. It's so rare that I let myself feed until my meal dies. So very rare that I meet someone who deserves it. I had forgotten how delicious it was. Knowing I wouldn't have to bother typing up a report? Perfection.

The Velveteen Machine

James Ebersole

It is midnight when I get home from work, remove my grease stained dress shirt, and fall back onto my bed. Exhausted after an open to close shift at some hole in the wall in Carytown, I must will myself into staying awake, convince myself that this rest is momentary, that the night is young and there is much work to be done, or rather work to begin. I hear the distant sound of a train passing through this rainy spring Richmond night, somewhere. "When this noise has passed," I tell myself, "I will open my eyes and get to writing."

Blood rushes to my head as I rise from the bed, and for a moment I am lost to the world, caught in a head rush daze. I remember when this was a fun sensation, back when I was a kid. Now it's something entirely different; a suggestion of a disconcerting loss of control. This is bad blood flow, this is someone slipping drugs into your drink, this is a bludgeon to the head, this is death. I put a pot of tea on the stove and log onto Facebook. Writing can wait until I've had some caffeine. I check some emails, see the date on my computer screen. May 2nd, 2011. May, oh month of May, how quickly you have come. Your first day is over, now your second day has taken the spotlight while your twenty nine other children wait their turn in the shadows of the wings.

I wish I would just write something, anything at all. There is an open call for submissions to a local horror anthology with a deadline of May 31st. The only requirement, besides a word limit, is that the story be set in Richmond. The capital of Virginia, where I currently reside, ranked one of the most dangerous cities in the country, former capital of the Confederacy, Poe's city. You'd think I'd be overflowing with stories to tell, but I just can't get anything to manifest itself. It is in this city that I've walked down narrow crooked alleys late at night, meandered through Hollywood Cemetery, passed through bad parts of town, gone for drinks in subculture bars with dangling plastic heads. But no matter where I go, or where I've been, inspiration is nowhere to be found.

One in the morning. The blinding vacuum of a blank word processor. I can't do this right now. I need fresh air, rain and all. I pick up my notebook and an umbrella, still damp, and walk out the front door.

On the Church Hill street I inhabit, one can typically see the skyline of the city of Richmond quite well. The rain hinders visibility a great deal tonight, however, and the lights of the high-rises are now faint smudges drifting through a velvety fog. All the pollen that had dusted the street earlier is now at the mercy of the water, and thick clumps of the yellow stuff gather around various puddles and gutters. I walk to an old haunt of mine that my friends simply call "the adult swings," though there is actually more to the location than that. This significant chunk of a city block used to be some sort of church activity center, but I've never known it as anything other than an abandoned building with an unkempt yard. The property is enclosed by a chain link fence. I pass through a part of the fence that has been knocked down and walk across a crumbling cement basketball court smothered in weeds. I notice the remains of a fire in the center. I don't understand why anyone would start a fire here. Being on this property is trespassing in a bad part of town, and why draw attention to a thing like that with flames? There is something else I notice on the ground all around the fire pile; little threads of fabric, swirling this way and that in the water. A few of these cling to my foot as I walk towards the swings.

Standing in a field of broken bottles and weeds, the swing set is rather tall, taller than any other I've ever seen. The heights one can reach when swinging here surpass any playground experience of my childhood. Kate says the scariest thing in the world is to close your eyes in the moment that you're suspended in the air and imagine you're dangling on the wings of an airplane. This makes for quite a rush of exhilaration, even for us jaded adults.

I select the swing farthest to the right and take a seat. The entire left side of the swing set is unusable. A fallen tree branch blocks the way, twisting dead around the weathered metal. I think about the tornadoes in Alabama. My sister told me of a woman who hid all of her children in the closet of her trailer while she herself stood in the doorway, prepared to use her body to shield them. A tree fell through the side of the trailer, ripping right through the walls of the closet, killing the children. The woman survived. Terrible things can happen anywhere.

Notebook in hand, looking at the spooky scene all around me, I have a thought. Why not set my story here? The atmosphere is suitable, and who knows what sort of inhabitants I could pencil into that abandoned building of which I have been too wary to explore. Rocking back and forth on the swing, I mindlessly raise my pencil and drop my pencil. Then raise and drop it again. Then again, as if putting the point to the paper enough times will eventually cause an idea to write itself. I focus on my surroundings, hoping to conjure what demons of inspiration may be found around me. Surely there is something to be discovered here. Yet the notebook page remains blank. It is hopeless. Worthless. I am nothing.

The rain stops. I begin to weep, unrestrained, as if all that water which fell so freely from the sky had been condensed into my skull and now had to settle for escaping into the world through my eyes. Ok, I need to pull myself together. There's still time. Suck it up and start writing. I wipe my eyes and get up to head home. That's when I see him, standing before me, wearing birds nest hair, a smile, and a floppy brown suit three sizes too big. He is a man I immediately recognize as someone I see in passing at least once a week.

"Aren't you the Carytown Clown?" I ask him. He laughs, his makeup covered face fully focused on me, and replies "That's me. Say, aren't you the Swing Set Sobber?"

"Just this once. I'm better known as the Carytown Waiter, or the Wannabe Writer."

"Ah. Carytown! Writer! So I see we work in similar areas, and in more ways than one. Tell me waiter-slash-writer, what's got you down tonight?"

I could dismiss the question and leave, but his intentions seem amiable, or at least harmless. I decide to confide in the Clown.

"It's just, well, you see, I'm working on putting something together for this upcoming horror fiction anthology. Small press, loose guidelines, short work, should be simple enough, right?

Thing is submissions are due the end of this month, and I still don't know where to start."

The clown's face contorts into a look of contemplation, or a mockery of such a look; I can't decide which. He then gives me the same words of encouragement that I've been deceiving myself with all night: "That still leaves you a whole month, right?"

"Yeah, sure, but in all honesty, I think the rest of the month's going to go by without me getting anywhere at the rate things are going."

"Nonsense! Not if you let me help you!" The Clown's shouting startles me, and he begins to talk with wild gesticulations. "Let me ask you this: have you ever written a horror story?"

I think back to all the straight faced literary poems and stories I've had the privilege of getting published.

"No" I say.

"That explains it all. Listen, listen, listen to me, in order to write a horror story you need a grasp of what it means to feel the touch of horror. Now, we all know horror stories rarely frighten, but they can unsettle, when done right. This means that you, as the writer, must be... unsettled. Now, I want you to swing for me. Yes, on the swing set little horror child. Just close your eyes, swing, and I will help you touch the terror of the possible."

The absurd direction the conversation has taken is beginning to dawn on me. "I don't see how a swing set is going to help my writing. Besides, what's a clown like you know what I'm going through?"

The Clown lets out an exaggerated gasp, clutches his heart, and begins to speak to me in a tone reminiscent of a king reminding his people that he is more important than any one of them. "Well, even if I'm just a clown, that still makes me a performance artist, and I must captivate passersby if I want to get paid. But, I'm not just a clown, that isn't all that defines me. I'm a writer, too, among other things."

"You write?"

"Of course! What's a street performing clown like me to do late at night, or when it rains? In rain, the makeup just smears, and no Carytown visitors want to stop for the show of a sad little drenched clown. No, I save my silly work for sunny days. But outside of this, I am something else entirely, a different creature, a force to be reckoned with as I've heard it said. Now, swing for me my fellow of Carytown and the written word. Swing, and I will, soon enough, open you to a world you never even saw coming."

I guess it's come to this, a decision to take the advice of a clown or go home. The memory of the torment of a blank page comes back to me. I begin to swing. Slowly at first, then gaining momentum and reaching heights that place me above the stranger in the brown suit, above the chain link fence. The clown tells me to close my eyes. I do this, and I'm on the wings of an airplane all over again.

"Now, I am going to read a story to you, it is a story I wrote, a horror story crafted this winter on those cold days when no one wanted to visit a lonely clown on Cary Street. All I want you to do is listen. Don't open your eyes. And keep swinging."

The clown begins to read his literary concoction to me in a murmur that is on the verge of being inaudible over the rush of wind in my ears. I manage to follow his narrative nonetheless.

* * *

"Everything comes in pairs. That is the structure of the universe. From polar opposites to Siamese Twins, two is all that is. The night, the day, the light, the dark. The day, the night, the dark ,the light. Light days and dark nights, and woe to those who stray from this. The world began with clear shining days and murk beyond black nights, always isolated from one another, coming and going in a synchronized ignorance. Things should've just stayed that way, but as humans became self aware and began to question the world around them (which was a mistake from the start), they took a fancy to the day, for it is then that things are easier observed and explained. These humans of an earlier world began to doubt the night, to shudder at the shroud of it all. They found themselves keeping awake, more and more, later and later, deeper into that blackness. It was then that humans first began their all-consuming attempts to illuminate the night. In the onslaught of bonfires and torches, the darkness yielded to the bastard lights and the humans fueling them. This went against the nature of things, and balance had to be restored. Just as day violated the night, darkness began to creep into the days. Shadows grew longer, and sometimes humans ventured into them and never came out. Search parties armed with stone spears searched for their missing companions, but those vanished were never to be found. The hunters that came close to these shadows could hear the whirring of a metal machine, an alien sound, for this was long before humans had ever even invented metal machines....."

* * *

The story seems more like a biblical parable than a work of

fanciful fabrication, not that I hold much distinction between these two things anyway. Yet I'm caught tangled in the yarn, which weaves tighter around me. I listen to the words of the story until the words melt away, and the swing set is gone, and what is there in place is nothing more concrete than a thread of physical and mental disorientation. I am sucked into the shadows of the story, and see the world not as the rock in space as I thought it to be, but rather a hideous thing composed of severed cartilage, slowly rotting away. I am soaring uncontrollably, and for the first time in my life I feel genuinely frightened. This fright turns to ecstatic joy, then becomes terror again, and so on and so on, flipping back and forth, like a month of nights and days condensed into a mere minute. Just as I feel that the two sensations are merging into one, to become the only emotion I'll ever feel again for the rest of my being, the words of the story stop, and I am back on the swing set in Church Hill.

Disoriented, I focus my vision on the clown, who is smiling and clapping his hands. "You did well writer, looking more inspired already. Now, leave this place. Go home to your computer and write. Sleep when you need to, but not before you've written *something*. But do rest up. Please. Meet me here tomorrow night, at midnight. Your training has just begun."

With nothing to say and seeing no other option, I go home and begin to write a story about a suicide curse unleashed upon a group of civil war veterans. I realize it's a pretty mediocre story from the start, but at least I'm writing something. I go to bed before the sun even rises, and wake up at two in the afternoon, groggy yet refreshed, four hundred words ahead of where I had been twelve hours ago. Not having to go to the restaurant today, I spend most of the day pounding out one word at a time, the time interspersed with daydreams of what will be in store for me come midnight.

I am one thousand words into the story when quarter to midnight comes. I leave my apartment and make for the swings, munching on a granola bar as I go, for I had not eaten all day. I arrive with minutes to spare. I keep on the lookout for the clown, hoping to see the direction he comes from to get an idea of where he lives. I miss this opportunity, for the clown is standing in front of me before I even realize he was approaching. He must have caught me in the middle of daydreaming about my work in progress. He pulls a book from his floppy suit jacket pocket and motions for me to start swinging. I do this as he reads to me. I lose myself to the words, just like last time, touching that fantastical sense of terror. When the story finishes, I return to reality and go home. Though I feel inspired, I find myself unable to write tonight, yet I rest easy, falling into a deep sleep, certain the swing set experience will help me in time. We continue these midnight meetings every night. The stories he reads to me, excluding that curious tale he presented the first night, are all works created by established, undisputed masters of the horror genre. I swing, while he reads to me Lovecraft, Blackwood, Ligotti - each night it is a story I had a familiarity with, but am now able to grasp the meaning of in a way I had never seen before. It is an experience so euphoric, so out of this world, that I find myself putting aside all cares of creating such stories of my own, and instead, eagerly awaiting the midnight telling of one to me.

My performance at my restaurant job is beginning to slip, and I don't even care. It is Tuesday, May 24th, one week before story submissions are due, when the manager pulls me aside for something. I think "surely I am to be fired." But what he says to me when we are finally alone is even more alarming; he is not firing me, but confiding in me, as if I were a friend. He is upset about something, this weasel of a man, this monster who has cheated me out of many a tip and has seemed to show nothing but hatred towards me from the start. He tells me that his wife, a miserably unattractive fat woman always hanging around the restaurant, has left him and taken their 10 year old son. My boss tells me he hasn't heard from them in days. He says that I am his favorite employee (this comes as a shock to me) and that he's closing up a bit early and needs someone to drink with. He says I'm "just the kind of company he needs" and that he'll pay for my drinks (more shocking words from a tip thief).

The boss and I end up drinking at some Shockoe Bottom bar adorned with tacky tiki torches. He sobs over a sunset margarita and three empty shot glasses while I awkwardly sip a mojito and stare at the floor.

"I can't go on like this anymore." He says to me. "It's like, everything is crumbling in front of me. My wife. My son. Gone. To who knows where. And the restaurant's on the rocks. Heck, you know this, I know you've seen me taking tips to help cover the bills. And I'm sorry for that, I really am. But it's just...it seems no one comes to Carytown anymore. Maybe it's this recession. But what I want to know is, where has all the tourism gone? It looks to me like the only people in Carytown these days are the business owners and street performers, both fighting to snatch up a buck."

At the mention of street performers I immediately think of the storytelling clown and check the time. It is 11:59 p.m.

"I have to leave." I say.

"What?"

"I have to leave." I repeat.

"Come on now, don't do that, you've barely finished your first drink."

"I'm sorry, but I have to go. I need to meet up with my girlfriend." I hope the lie convinces him, but it only seems to stir up his rage, as if me meeting with my girl reminds him that he will, eventually, need to go home to an empty house tonight.

"Fine then, vanish on me, just like the rest. Don't bother coming to work tomorrow. You're fired." I nod, say something about not minding getting off a sinking ship, and run out the door. Being a good dozen blocks away from the meeting spot, I curse letting my boss drive me and not insisting on riding my bike to the bar. I sprint as fast as I can, but it is already 12:04 when I finally find myself back in Church Hill, collapsing onto a swing, and panting for my life.

After I catch my breath and realize no one else is here I take a seat on a balance beam in the yard, thinking that to sit on a swing without the clown's presence was now some act of sacrilege. Where is he? Did he already come, grow impatient, and decide to go home? No, surely he hasn't abandoned me. Perhaps he walked to the store for a snack to kill time. Even a clown's gotta eat, right? I decide to wait it out until one o'clock. If he doesn't come by one, then I'll go home, maybe work on my story. It won't be the end of the world, and I can explain what happened tomorrow. I'm sure he'll understand. I could even show up early, since I won't be shackled down to working the restaurant anymore.

So I sit on the balance beam, waiting. I find myself staring at that eerie abandoned building I've been told to avoid at all costs.

I've heard talk of homeless squatters living in there, homeless people of the deranged, desperate, and violent variety. I have always been skeptical of the presence of such individuals here, for the building has always seemed dead and silent to me, like the lingering bones of a long since decayed corpse. Yet tonight I'm starting to believe in the rumors I've heard, for although the building looks to be empty, in the silence of the night I can hear the faint sounds of some activity within.

I stand up and walk away from the balance beam, creeping, cautious step by wary step, towards that dilapidated structure. The sound I hear as I am arm's length from the caved-in doorway is now unmistakable; what I'm hearing is the whirring of some machine. I step into the darkness of the building, a deeper darkness than that of the night around me, and follow the sound to wherever it leads. Tripping over scraps of mildewed cloth and broken bottles, I make my way down the hallway dead to sight and cut a right into the opening of the room from which the sound emits.

The space before me is cast in a dim silken glow that is a sight both noxious and beautiful to witness, as if the air were some delicate cloth drenched in odorless, luminescent venom. My eyes take a moment to adjust to this and take in the scene before me. Immediately recognizable is the degree of clutter in the room. Jumbled about in haphazard stacks is an assortment of musical instruments, makeup, paints, canvases, sketch pads, playing card decks, handkerchiefs, and, in greater abundance than anything else, spools of fabric. I walk through this wall of things, trying to reach the source of the sound on the other side of the room. It is difficult passage, for as soon as I push one thing aside two more things fall in its place. Initially my aim was to investigate the room without leaving a trace of my presence, but with my patience tried and my nervous curiosity boiling over, I end up trampling over all the stuff, bounding through the room, the sound of splattered paints and breaking guitar strings beneath my feet. I eventually break free from the hoarded clutter and tiptoe to the end of that long and narrow room. By this point, the only things stacked around me are empty fabric spools stripped bare of any cloth. The machine sound has grown louder, but the strange limitation to my vision brought on by the lighting of the room still obscures the source of the sound. There is also another sound, which I can only describe as the sound of hundreds of coins being sorted and sifted. I step forward, and see that's exactly what I'm hearing.

Before me is a large satchel of coins, being funneled into some sort of rubber hosing. I advance, searching for what the hose is connected to, and there it is, the source of that mechanical sound. The Machine hisses and writhes before me. It is the size of a small car, moving with artificial automation, yet in a way that vaguely resembles the movements of a mammalian organism capable of thought. The thing is made up of what looks to be a combination of tarnished silver, fur covered flesh most resembling the hide of a black bear, and occasional patches of cloth stitched into this flesh. I can only reason that the machine is equal parts organic and inorganic.

The end of the rubber hose is connected to a gap in the flesh, which is protected by a thick glass dome. The coins from the satchel are fed into this hole, and are expelled into a large trunk situated at a similar, yet uncovered, hole on the opposite side of the Machine. I watch this process happen with jaw unhinged, until the sound of shifting coins stops. The holes are blocked up by a pink fleshy membrane, and the machine makes a screeching sound that seems to emulate the excited squeal of a little girl discovering an Easter Egg for her wicker basket. Then a hatch in the metal opens, and a spool of cloth within the Machine begins to unravel. Dozens of tiny silver appendages begin to weave the cloth at an incredible speed. This cloth begins to take form. A human form. The Machine spits out its creation, a featureless "doll" (for lack of a better word) the size of a 10 year old boy. Then the silver arms are at it again, this time working on something of a larger mass. This second creation only takes a few seconds longer than the first, and soon enough the Machine unleashes the second form, which has the shape of obese femininity that I immediately recognize as the body shape of my boss' wife.

I run from the Machine, crossing the room and its sea of clutter. I pass through the doorway and into the hall as the sound of coins being sorted resumes behind me. I make it outside and want only to flee from this place, to leave Richmond and never return. But this desire comes too late. He is here, approaching me, rolling up the sleeves of an oversized brown blazer.

"You'll have to pardon the lateness of my arrival" the Clown says to me in that grandiose way of his. "I've been in Carytown, collecting coins to feed to the Velveteen Machine!"

The clown shuffles closer to me. I realize he has not come alone. There are others, street performers of the night, stepping out of the shadows, coming up the streets from all different directions. As they get closer, I begin to recognize some of them, these familiar faces of Carytown. The magician, thin as the cards he does tricks with. The wisened blind man who juggles his two glass eyes. The balding, pot-bellied mime. The girl with no arms who creates paper flowers with her feet. Musicians with banjos, accordions, hammered dulcimers, and a thousand folk songs in their heads. They begin to converge around the hole in the fence, cross through and approach us, like a slow marching parade.

The clown puts his hands on my shoulder. I stagger back from the touch of his sticky hands. "Judging from where you just came from, I take it you and the Machine have already met. Good! We've been waiting a long time for someone new, someone like you. The Machine has expressed much interest in the prospect, right from the start. We all have."

I feel a dozen pair of arms (and a single pair of feet) lifting me up from the ground, stifling my struggles to break free, carrying me to the swing set.

"And now the time has finally arrived for you to leave behind this pitiful day by day, job by job life of yours to become something new, something antihuman. Stop squirming now, you can't escape this. You have been shackled to this one purpose since the first time you shed all human inhibitions and tasted the nightmare of the truth, that first night on the swings. I would even say you were born for this, if not for the fact that you never should have been born at all. No one should have. This is something we aim to correct."

I am forced into the swing opposite my usual, the one rendered unusable by the fallen tree. The many hands hold me down and begin to rock me around.

"Swing for me writer, swing, swing, and let it slip away, let yourself slip away. Let the rapids of the terror of being undone engulf you, and may they wash you out to that tranquil still dark sea beyond, whose waves whisper all the truths of this hideous twisting universe."

I am forced to swing, a multitude of sticky hands pushing my back, propelling me further and further up. I realize I am getting closer to the tree branch with each swing, yet the moment of impact never comes, and the tree branch begins to float away, beyond the rusted metal frame, drifting off into the night. The stars begin to blur together and the faces of the mimes and musicians and freaks all slip away. Once more I am there, immersed in that perfect and joyous horror. Only this time it is not the stories of a clown taking me there, but the constant whispers of the Velveteen Machine as its creaking voice begins to undo me and weave me into something new.

In the beginning there are flashes of the mundane, a momentary return to a human existence. The first time this happens with any lasting clarity, I notice there are two children on the swings beside me. I try to shout for them to save me, but they seem not to hear. I cast my eyes down to the sun-bathed grass below me and distinctively see the shadow of a fallen tree branch, as if it were still there. I also note that although the shadows of the children can be seen, there is no shadow of my own, no form at all sitting in the shadow of a still and empty swing beneath a fallen tree branch. I drift away into that other being again, and the last cohesive vision I have as seen through something resembling human sight is the image of all those freakish street show performers piling up, then setting fire to, the lifeless velveteen forms that were once two little children who inhabited the swings beside me.

What have I become? I once had I girlfriend I cared about. But that doesn't matter anymore. I don't even remember her name. Do I even remember my own name? I realize now I have completely lost myself and know nothing of time. Surely submissions for a horror anthology in which I once aspired to be published have closed, the deadline long past. But that doesn't matter anymore. I am beyond that now. My writing has found a new home, a new purpose.

I can see myself now, wandering the sidewalks outside of shops, reciting my poetry and prose to anyone who will listen. "Would you like to buy a chapbook of poems sir? Only seventy five cents, just give me those coins, the right coins, the ones that share the same birth year as you. That's how the Velveteen Machine works these days, you see. All it needs is the date you were born to make you unborn. No, no, don't leave! I can save you, I can save all of you human monsters. This is a better fate than death, you see, to slip into that velvety dark sea, where we all cease to be."

To be a servant of the Velveteen Machine means to transcend your human mortality. Still, I realize that eventually the Velveteen Machine will have converted all whom it could not devour, and its hunger will turn on us one day. As death was once unavoidable, this is a fate I know I can not escape when the time comes. Yet, instead of having any sense of dread or nervousness, I am only comforted by this fact. The thought of being one of the final privileged few to remain after the culling keeps me going; gives me hope for what I will become when I stop swinging. Who knows, maybe I could be the very last one. I could flee the Machine, live in the Amazon, the Sahara, or some other dense wilderness, all alone. But the Machine would catch up to me eventually. Too cheat this fate will not be my final plan, for others will surely be thinking of trying the same thing and will undoubtedly be the first to fall. Instead I will bide my time, strive to last long enough to see the world unpeopled. Then, staring out across that empty silent world, in that moment before I surrender myself to the Machine, I will finally know what it means to be entirely alone.

The human population is numbered in the billions, and whether or not I can manage to outlast them all is yet to be seen. All I know is that there is much work to be done before that final day comes. The Velveteen Machine speaks to me now, in gurgles and creaks, telling me I will soon be ready to step down from these swings. I will become a Shepard of men, to lead the anomaly that is humankind to its rightful oblivion. I will come down to this world, transformed, and show you all what horror means.

231 Creeper

Phil D. Ford

Alyssa woke up screaming from the explosion in her house, or dream, or both. The bed sheets were damp, her eyes wallowed with tears and she couldn't quite figure out why. It was October 2nd, the week before her friend Emily was to get married. She looked at the clock.

12:16PM.

Some friends were back in town for the wedding and had decided that last night was to be a late evening. There were many drinks involved.

"Mmph." Alyssa perhaps had been a little too happy to see all of her old friends again. She got up to pee.

As she sat on the cold bowl, she tried to sit up straight, her head bobbled from side to side, her eyes pulsed in their lids. Recalling the events of last night, the martinis at Sette, the crawl up to 3 Monkeys, the shots at Avalon, she also remembered the plan.

"Lunch. Right." She was to meet the smaller circle of girlfriends at Willow Lawn for a late lunch. The four of them agreed to it last night. What time was that again?

"Two?" She held that thought for a moment then nodded. Time to get ready.

Alyssa had known this group since past forever; college, first jobs all waitressing together, first marriages, divorces. Over the years, she had started to see them less and less, and frankly, they were drifting apart. The connection of youth was no longer a needed ingredient to her make-up and the relationships were almost starting to feel forced. Hell, she was nearly forty, and this was Emily's third attempt to marry a man and not wind up completely annoyed by his bad habits.

That's mean, she thought, you love Emily. She is like your sister; I mean you are the closest to her out of all of them. Maybe you're just jealous because you have no one in your life. Maybe. Besides, her weddings are usually a good time.

"Hangover talk." What the hell was that damn dream anyway? Explosions? Graves? Crypts?

Graveyard.

In the dream Alyssa was walking down along the roadside, checking the names on each stone, each crypt; Kuper, Worthington, Lyons –why? A bitter wet wind swept up from the river through the narrow asphalt road and slithered through the gravestones like an aggressive copperhead.

Hollywood.

"That's where I was." The nightmare was becoming more vivid now as she got through her morning routine. The coffee was especially helpful.

She sat at her small first floor kitchen nook looking out over the alley courtyard between Grove and Hanover Avenues. This little off-shoot room from the galley kitchen completely sold her on the house. She loved the way the morning sunshine flooded in the two windows at an angle and lit the rest of the kitchen.

Sometimes she didn't even need the light on. Alyssa was instantly smitten when the realtor showed her this nook; the small door to the side led to a modest porch, perfect for the hammock in summer.

The whole place was really a charmer when she was looking to buy her first house ten years ago. All of her mid century chic furniture somehow complimented the arts and craft style. Built in the nineteen teens, it shared heat with the neighbors in the winter, and allowed the cross breeze to flow in summer when she opened all the windows. Sure, it needed its fair share of work, but she took to the quaint craftsmanship immediately. The front living room was met by the stairway leading up to the bedroom, office and bath, showing off the wooden stair banister carved by hand in that familiar clamshell shape. The swell curvature of picture molding all around the living and dining rooms, and the swirled green and grey tile of the fireplace were a testament to an earlier time. Alyssa appreciated every bit of it. This house was her security, her nest, and that nook, boy, that sold her pretty damn quickly.

The dream though, something was pulling her back to it.

Right, she thought, I was there alone on a cold and windy wet day. It sounds almost cookie-cutter...silly.

She tried to analyze the reason why she dreamed about Hollywood Cemetery; on TV, maybe, or talked about last night while out drinking. Maybe there was a flash pan conversation with Emily that sparked her mind to think of the Poole Crypt or that stupid Richmond Vampire myth. A newsreel of yesterday's events ran in her mind. She thought about that part in the dream when...

Shit, was there no reason?   She woke up yelling and dripping in sweat, that's intense. There has to be a reason.

A chill, slow and meticulous, starting from the bottom of her spine, crawled up her back and spread out over her shoulders. At first she thought it was an insect or spider, briefly, then it tingled at the base of her skull and she knew better. Her hand trembled and the cup of hot coffee she held spilled on her fingers. She practically didn't notice due to the other sensation she was feeling. It was calling, an explosion of her will to investigate. Go there, find something.

"Really? Now?" Alyssa sighed aloud and looked at the vintage aqua clock on the kitchen wall. It was almost one. There was still time. She knew this feeling would not go away until she went there, to the cemetery. If anything it would put her at ease.

"Okay, fine, I'll go." A quick trip to Hollywood it was going to be. Settle the curiosity; maybe even a spark would ignite to remind her why she had this terrible dream. Maybe it would satiate the nagging wonder; maybe it would shake her nerves free of it.

An eerie feeling came over Alyssa when she parked in the space across from the Cemetery building. She got out of her car and looked around. Her senses had sharpened, every detail of the lush ivy in the old stone wall entrance stood out with bold shadows and dark green angles. A wren scolded her as she passed by down the street. She could almost smell the mustiness of the crypts across the small valley of holly and cedar.

It's funny how significant historical places in your own town, that people travel miles to visit, you never give much thought. Alyssa hadn't been here in years. She strolled passed the confederate officers arch, robins darted away from her frantically, she thought about the mold on the arch, how it needed some cleaning, or if the aged look was more suitable for the dead of a lost cause.

Construction.

Approaching the bottom of the hill at the turn, she saw fresh red clay in large mounds and two midsized bulldozers perched on either side. Alyssa was concerned at first, that maybe a casket had been turned up or worse. For some reason she thought of genocide and the image of hundreds of bodies being pushed into large dirt graves by metal machines.

Dispelling the grim thought quickly led Alyssa to one of the last times she was here. She was nineteen, maybe twenty, with some of her college friends trying to sneak in this very corner in the middle of the night. Emily was there, and so was her first husband, Richard.

A group of them were hanging out after the evening Sociology class. Richard was renting one of those row houses across the street from campus. Usually five or six of them got together afterward; sometimes it was a study session, other times they drank till the thick of the morning. That particular night, and maybe it was because Finals were over and the cheap beer brought on some bravado, they came up with the idea. Who doesn't think about creeping around there when you are young, adventurous and full of booze like that? It wasn't too long of a walk to Oregon Hill from Harrison Street, so they headed over to the corner where a hole in the wire fence was supposed to be.

Unfortunately, the hole was boarded up, so they decided to bail on the idea and walk down by the train tracks to watch the sunrise instead. Alyssa remembered them all sitting on the railroad embankment at the bottom of the hill. Emily and Richard were being all lovey-dovey wretchedness, quietly kissing and whispering stupid things to each other every so often. She listened to the river sounds, most everyone was quiet by that point, dozing from the all-nighter or enjoying the calmness as well. There was serenity, a certain peacefulness, in the view as the sun peaked behind the trees down river. It was an etched memory. It had given her a warm feeling, like she had always been here. As the bright sun rose higher, she looked back toward the Cemetery, and thought just for a moment that she saw other people in there, dancing or twirling around headstones, maybe they had found another way in, and then they were gone in a blink of an eye.

"Wow, that was a long time ago." Alyssa said to herself. She smiled a little, seeing the railroad tracks just beyond the upturned piles of clay, and shook her head out of the memory. That still wasn't an answer to the dream.

Where was that crypt? Was it the Poole crypt? Yes. Alyssa rounded the turn and made her way back up the hill. There were so many interesting graves around. Even though she hadn't been to this place in such a long time, she remembered one of the great things about Hollywood is that you can always find something you've never noticed before. An odd statue, some aligned symbols on a headstone, the death dates of a married couple being the same day only thirty years later, there was a stillness vibe to the place. Cars and people drifted by her in the background so seamlessly that it felt as if everything here paced itself in slow motion. The rest of the world was flying by, practically spinning off the planet, but here, things barely moved.

An abrupt sense of being watched hit her. At first she tried to blame a breeze, maybe the same cold breeze in her dream, but nothing was moving around her. Alyssa looked ahead again for the car that had just passed but it was long gone to the far side of the cemetery. She was alone here. She looked at the crypt to her left, it was the infamous Poole.

Somehow a legend was born that this was where the Richmond Vampire resided. In the early twentieth century, some railroad workers were in a train tunnel in Church Hill, the engine exploded and buried them. The legend had it that a specter crawled from the collapsed tunnel and ran madly across town, being chased by people, and supposedly took up residence here.

Alyssa rolled her eyes. Bullshit tales. She really knew the story derived from one of the victims, Benjamin Mosby, whose skin was so badly burned in the disaster that he died later that evening. Knowing the answer to the legend still didn't really stave off her anxiousness.

This burial was in need of repair. It almost represented all the spooky rumors it received. The unkempt shrub that curled over the concrete ledge above the door, the built up grime in the name and date of the keystone, the two iron columns all that remained of an iron fence now rusted away. Alyssa walked closer, trying to peer in.

Touching the contour on the grey stone archway leading to the door was as cold as the feeling on the back of her neck. The iron bars on the gate of the outer door were starting to rust at the top.

There was a lone faded rose tied there by someone, probably from a few weeks ago. She wondered who. The plaster walls on the other side were eroding, revealing the brick underneath and making red dust on the ground like anthills. The small solid door to the inner crypt was rusted with a half inch crevice opening at the edge. A few of the bars to the inner crypt had rusted away entirely and the windows were broken out, allowing a strained view inside. She leaned in more, her forehead pressing against the bars of the outer door. Her eyes narrowed, adjusting to the darkness in the actual crypt.

Something moved.

Surely a squirrel inside the window ledge. No. It's larger, with more intention. Wait. There's a hand. Fingers flat, prying through the crevice of the inner crypt door, trying to find purchase, to open and get through.

Alyssa let out a gasp, at same time a hiss reverberated from the crypt, she fell back.

"What the fuck?" She stumbled, turning to catch herself from the fall, landing on her hands with the Poole Crypt behind her, over her, looming like a haunted obelisk. She gripped the concrete with her fingers, her legs like wheels spinning in place, moved her forward and up toward the road. It felt like a mouse dream, the hawk swooping down for its prey, the vision suddenly gone as she heard a car come from the other side of the small valley.

Alyssa straightened up, and walked to the road. She watched the car drive around the bend by the construction area and thought how absurd she must have looked to them. Her heart was still racing. Was that real? She cautiously looked back to crypt.

Nothing.

"Crazy." She chuckled, but it was nervous and forced. She looked at her watch; she had already missed the lunch date. It was almost four.

"What the hell?" She didn't believe it, couldn't believe it. How could I have been here nearly three hours?

She started walking back to the car and pulled out her cell. Two messages. Alyssa didn't have to check who they were from. It was Emily. Clearly, lunch was missed, which was fine because she suddenly wasn't feeling well. Maybe last night's potions were giving her the hint to take it easy right now. Maybe it was something else. No matter what is was, she decided not to call Emily. She needed a change of scenery. Bev's Ice Cream in Carytown sounded good right now despite her nausea.

"That sounds like a plan." Alyssa put the key in the car door and looked back to the crypt. For a brief moment she thought she saw the outer door open and something come out. Then she thought of the people dancing in the cemetery at sunrise twenty years ago. A brief wave of panic rose from her chest as she started the car and got the hell out of there.

Alyssa decided to walk to Carytown from her house. The fresh air would do some good and she could take the bus back. Bev's Ice Cream seemed to be doing pretty well despite the crisp evening air. She sat by the large front window with a cup of Dirty Chocolate. Dirty Chocolate was the best. It was a rich complex taste without feeling too dense or that she had eaten an entire quart. The girl that scooped it for her was surprised they still had some this late in the day. It's a damn popular flavor.

This spot was great for watching people; the scruffy young kid slamming on his claw hammer banjo for coin, the trendy skinny girls with hoop earrings and funky shoes blabbing on cell phones, the parents with their college aged hipster son walking into the New York Deli for dinner. The shopping district always felt to be moving and Alyssa imagined a centipede squirming down a well beaten path. She checked her cell again. Five messages. Maybe she will just call Emily tomorrow, when her mood wasn't so weird and foreboding.

Alyssa looked down into the cup of her ice cream and noticed the edges in the bottom were starting to puddle with chocolate. She thought of that hand coming through the door of the crypt, trying to get out. Was there blood on the fingers? It all happened so fast. She stabbed at the melted edged with her spoon. Were there even fingernails on that hand? Ripped off at the cuticles with fresh bleeding. She couldn't quite remember.

Looking out of the window again, seeing all the movement and activity, Alyssa thought about that crypt door opening when leaving the cemetery. Did something really get out or was it a trick of the eye? An omen? Is something telling her about Emily's wedding? That's absurd.

The sun was setting and shadows fell, casting long dark corners on the storefronts, street and sidewalks. Her gaze languidly scanned the shops across the street. There was a strange figure in the window of the New York Deli. A darkness, like a blur, she couldn't quite make it out. It was moving toward the restaurant entrance, in her direction. Was it the dusk approaching or her age, a need for glasses? Goose bumps slid up the backs of her arms from the elbows to her shoulders and neck.

She then felt darkness behind her, like the feeling of a storm coming when walking in a field. The sudden drop in temperature, the way a few bits of rain plop on your head, cold and running down your back, but this was distinctively different. It felt like a person was there, some leering sycophant, reaching out to touch. She turned quickly to see what it was.

It was nothing, really, only the ice cream girl wiping some tables a few feet away.

"Everything all right?" The girl asked.

"Sure." Alyssa replied, but she wanted to go home now more than ever before.

Dusk had approached while she stood at the bus stop. The thing about waiting for the bus, Alyssa mused, was that you always waited at least ten minutes, whether it was on time or not.

There was a man sitting on the bench near Alyssa who was not quite with it. She had seen him around before. He was one of those regular homeless gentlemen that pick up cigarette butts off the street to finish the last leaves of tobacco. He would probably be better suited in some kind of adult day care situation if only the city could afford it. After she arrived and did not have any cigarettes to offer, the man went back to his business of having some dialog with himself about bus schedules. She had a hard time knowing that he was not talking to her.

Alyssa looked toward the oncoming traffic and said, "Ah, this one is mine." The man kind of gave her a knowing look, like he knew the whole time that it would be. The bus airbrakes hissed as it pulled to the curb. The door opened in front of her, and inside it was practically empty.

The homeless man watched as Alyssa paid her fare and sat at a window seat in the middle. The bus merged into traffic. Curiously he saw a blurred grey image seated directly behind the girl. The image turned toward him, and seemed to grin. Only there were no eyes, no nose, no lips. There was no manner of facial distinction for a man, woman, or anything. It was a smudge, like when someone moves too fast when getting their picture taken. Whatever it was that was sitting behind that woman who got on the bus, it had no face.

She threw open the door, shutting herself in from the rest of the world with a click of the deadbolt. Alyssa was happy to be home.

"I could use a drink, then bed." Booze, pajamas and sleep were sometimes her cure-all for crappy days.

Walking across the living room, she didn't notice or feel the presence by the fireplace. Her mind was on the comforts of the house, the kitchen at night as she poured herself a stiff one. Alyssa also didn't notice the figure behind her the whole time as she sat at the dining room table sipping her bourbon, thinking about the day.

"Madness," she snickered. "Here I am blowing off my friend during her wedding week." She laughed to herself, "Well, it *is* her third. Cheers to you, Em."

As she raised her glass in the air toasting no one, a feeling came over her again and she paused. Her eyes widened to look in the window across the room in front of her. It was dark outside; no alley lights were on so she could see the reflection of the dining room where she sat. She could almost make out a figure behind her a few feet away, raising a hand as if toasting as well.

Alyssa was frozen. Her breath heavy, her chest moved faster.

"Who's there?" She pleaded and turned to see with all the courage she could muster.

Nothing was there.

She let out a sigh and kicked back the rest of the bourbon, the soothing heat down her throat a therapeutic welcome.

"Screw this day then. It's bedtime."

She went upstairs to the bedroom and found her favorite comfortable Fall pajamas, a flannel set with some poodle prints all over. Alyssa didn't even like dogs really, particularly poodles. It was a bit of a silly gift from an old boyfriend a few years ago and the best thing he ever gave her. They were plenty warm and the material was no longer itchy like flannel can sometimes feel. They were just the right thing for her now.

Alyssa pulled down her bed sheets, then went to the bathroom and brushed her teeth. It was already starting to feel like the regular going to bed routine. The dream was being further left behind as an odd memory, bad vibes, something she drank that put her in a bad mindset. What was that drink at that bar again?

"Not doing that one anymore." She said spitting a mouthful of paste into the sink. "You're getting too old."

Alyssa slid into bed; the cool sheets a welcome comfort. She loved how she could stretch her whole body out under the covers and feel every bit of chill in the fabric, knowing that at any moment, the flannel and her body heat would be making the whole bed toasty and she would more than likely flail something off in the middle of the night. She thought about reading a little, but instead just stared up at the ceiling with the nightstand light on.

Alyssa yawned, and then stretched her arms above her head feeling the wall with her fingertips. She turned off the light then settled back onto her pillow in the darkness.

Wait.

Her arms trembled, the skin on her head tensed and wrinkled with fear. What was that in the corner by the dresser just now?

A figure.

Its head was hung low, as if ashamed or angry, she couldn't tell. It wasn't like a man. It was an apparition, a smear, but its features angled in the shadows, its face grey with hollow detail.

Alyssa let out a gasp, trying to talk to whatever was in the room with her that was standing there waiting, maybe approaching the bed.

"Leave," was all she could whimper. "Please."

Alyssa lay in pitch black for what seemed like forever, paralyzed, wondering when the creature would be upon her. A minute went by, then five, then ten. Nothing happened. She must be crazy.

No, I'm turning on the light.

Nervous with anticipation as to what she would really see, she leaned over and clicked on her light then looked in the corner.

There was her dresser.

She released a deep sigh.

"Okay, good night." She turned off the light again and lay there in the stillness. Alyssa felt more exhausted, like she could sleep a hundred years. Her hands reached down and out under the sheets just like before, just like she'd done time and time again at bedtime.

Her breath stopped short. As she reached her left hand across the mattress, another hand met hers in the bed. It was cold, colder than anything she'd ever felt before; wet with blood and loose flesh at the fingertips. It grasped her hand in a bond that would take her to the moment that would forever answer the question of dream and reality as well as sanity and madness.

Alyssa was holding hands with a specter.

Gamble's Hill

Daniel Gibbs

One of the few bright spots about the Westchester, Chad decided—picking the pizza flyers out of his real mail—was that it was remarkably roach-free. All of his Sig Ep brothers, who lived scattered among the old houses nearby, were surrounded by a veritable National Guard unit of gigantic roaches. And, he thought, it wasn't like he was clean or anything. In recent memory, he'd pulled a pair of boxers off the laundry pile, applied the sniff test, and was about to re-wear them before realizing that there was a stray bit of egg roll stuck in them. His brother Morris, a weirdly neat Chem major, lived in a building so infested that his pet iguana couldn't keep up with the wildlife.

Otherwise, Westchester was a dump. It was at least eighty years old. Its plumbing had a nasty habit of... well, it had a *lot* of nasty habits. It leaked, but when you wanted to shower, it refused to cooperate. The toilet either overflowed or it wouldn't flush at all. As for the kitchen, everything in it was an antique. The refrigerator was right out of a Little Rascals movie, with one of those big drum-type things on top. There was only one outlet in the kitchen, and his new microwave kept overloading the fuse.

Still, it was cheap, and only three blocks from most of his classes. Also, it was quiet. Most of the other apartments seemed to be occupied by old people, and the other one on his floor wasn't occupied at all. After a pretty disastrous sophomore GPA, Chad couldn't afford to flag any more classes, so the quiet apartment kept him away from any unintentional partying.

Before he could get to the staircase, the door to one of the first floor apartments popped open. Chad instantly regretted having stopped to sort his mail; old Mrs. Mitchell gave him the willies. In the month since he'd moved into the Westchester, the old woman had made a point of cornering him whenever she saw him. She was always nice, but she had a weird tic, and her left eye wandered.

"I'm just wonderin', Mr. Lennon, how you like your apartment now that you've been here a while?"

"Just fine, thank you Miz Mitchell..." Chad shuffled, eager to escape the old lady's bath ramblings. She was strangely in love with the crumbling apartment building. Last week, she'd rattled on for nearly half an hour about it, talking about the beautiful furniture that used to sit in the lobby and the fireplace and the big fish tank that had once been there. When she'd gone off on that description, Chad couldn't help looking around to see that the lobby's mosaic floor now held nothing but more pizza flyers and dead leaves that had blown in over the last winter.

"I moved in here when I was a bride, you know." Chad snapped back to alertness, as the old woman had just laid her gloved hand on his shoulder. She seemed perpetually dressed for a garden party, though he'd never seen her leave the apartment.

He knew that some sort of reply was needed, and not knowing what else to say, he muttered "I'm sure you musta been a beautiful bride!" It was the right answer; what passed for a girlish blush came over the sunken cheeks.

"You'll make a fine groom someday!"

Chad, now thoroughly creeped-out, made a quick excuse about needing to study and jogged upstairs to his apartment, where he promptly slipped in a pile of dog puke and fell flat on his ass.

Chivas the dog had been incredibly annoying over the past few weeks. He'd taken to overeating and then promptly vomiting. Usually a cheerful, independent dog, he'd also taken to attaching himself to Chad at every possible moment. While he wasn't used to the dog's newfound clinginess, Chad didn't really mind that much. He loved his pet and found him a welcome companion now that he was forcing himself into a monastic lifestyle of constant studying.

Chad (and Chivas, draped over his chest) woke to the dulcet tones of the WRVA morning news. This meant - being a Tuesday - that it was time for his most completely useless class.

VCU's academic policies insist that all students must be well-rounded in spite of themselves. Thus, it comes to pass, at VCU, that neo-Gothic art students find themselves forced to play volleyball in gym classes, and accounting majors find themselves studying "Lost Architecture in Richmond, Virginia."

As bullshit classes went, Chad had to admit that this one wasn't too bad—at the very worst, there was nothing more to do than show up for class and look at slides of buildings that had been gone for three decades. On the flipside, looking at pictures of the Capitol Theatre and abandoned Baptist churches ate up three hours every week, which meant a course overload, since he needed to re-take two of last year's failed classes.

At the beginning of his junior year, Chad Lennon had come to the unpleasant realization that he needed to—as his father would surely say—"buckle down." Two years earlier, he had arrived in Richmond, confident that the road to a good job and a nice car would be as simple as it had been in his suburban Washington high school. His workaholic parents, a research chemist and a patent lawyer, rarely saw their son during his high school years, but spent a fair amount of effort impressing upon him the need to "make something of himself."

The elder Lennons had indeed made something of themselves. The son of a garage mechanic and the daughter of a grocer, both had been the type of student who worked only for the sake of grades and went out for sports only for the sake of padding college applications and later, resumes. Neither could understand the easygoing son who played football because it was fun, and ended up at VCU instead of aggressively pursuing admission to a more prestigious school. It certainly hadn't set well with them when Chad pledged Sig Ep, though Mr. Lennon the Elder had to admit that fraternal bonds might eventually create good business contacts. Chad's parents did, in fact, motivate him to improve his grades henceforth—not from any desire to heed them, but with every intention of having a life far different from theirs.

After feeding a whining Chivas, Chad made his way out of the Westchester and headed for class. He narrowly avoided Mrs. Mitchell, whose door peeped open as he crossed the lobby and bolted through the doors. Though he was on time for class, he found the room already full. These art students took their classes very seriously. He beelined to the last seat available, next to a girl dressed in art-girl-stereotype black, who wasted no time in glaring disparagingly at his fraternity letter shirt and madras shorts.

After only a few class sessions, Chad had developed distaste for the professor, Thelma Ritter. An insistently tweedy sort, she made it clear that the only use she had for Virginia at all lay in its past. While gushing over the Old Dominion's colonial history, she was careful to maintain her status as an outsider, and at that one more clearly qualified to discuss Richmond's past than its own citizens could be. She pointedly pronounced the neighboring county's name as "Hen-Ree-Ko" and gave "Manchester" the clipped British pronunciation that surely hadn't been heard in Virginia since Jefferson's time.

Since the professor had rattled on considerably about "adaptive reuse" of buildings, the announcement of the project came as no surprise: students would team up, pick a demolished building, research its history, and provide an argument for why it should have been saved. This struck Chad as a pretty obvious ploy: the professor just wanted to use her students as research slaves for her own efforts to publish. Unfortunately, she also assigned the teams herself, and stuck Chad with the condescending art chick in the next seat.

The art chick let out an exasperated sigh and rolled her eyes. She asked, "Do you even know what adaptive reuse *is*?" Chad was stunned. Her condescension hadn't really surprised him, but her outright rudeness did. Still, he couldn't think of much to say, so he tried to be polite.

"Actually, I do—like turning the old Capitol Garage building into student housing."

She indulged in a contemptuous giggle. "It's just not the sort of thing I'd expect a frat boy to know."

That did it. "You were wrong, then. But I *would* expect an art student to know how to take a shower, so it looks like we were *both* wrong about something."

"Oh, my GOD!" The art chick's mouth dropped.

"Hey, you started off by insulting me. What did you expect?"

"If I didn't have so much respect for Professor Ritter, I'd walk out of here right now."

"I'm not surprised that you respect her so much, you're just as condescending and elitist as she is."

"You are *unreal.*"

Chad laughed. "I probably am, especially if being real means having to wear black turtlenecks and patchouli-stink in August, but we have to do this damn project..."

The art chick finally caved. "I give up. You're an ass, but we do have to do this. I'm Willow, by the way."

"Of course you are. I'm Chad. So, were your parents hippies too? Or did *you* decide that your name is Willow?"

"And of course your name would be Chad. Isn't every fratboy douchebag named Chad or Josh?"

"I was named for my grandfather, and he wasn't a fraternity man. He didn't go to college."

"Well, really, my name is Eugenie, but I hate it."

"Because your parents wanted something French."

"No, because my mother loved *Gone With the Wind*. I'm lucky that I didn't get pitched off a horse just to complete her fantasy."

Chad took a moment to digest this. At this point, it would be a little bit painful to admit that he'd not only read, but enjoyed *Gone With the Wind*. Why destroy this girl's horrible image of him now?

"So, uh, Nature Girl..."

"Willow."

"I might just go with Eugenie. It's not as silly."

"You really *are* unreal."

"So says the girl who won't use her real name."

The class ended, and Chad was able to make his way to the more congenial atmosphere of statistics class. It was good to be in a familiar place. Stats presented a good contrast to Lost Architecture—hard facts, and no judgmental girls who'd invented their own names. After class, Chad ambled over to Bogart's for a much-needed beer. He had just unpacked his notebook when his phone rang.

It was Jim Morris, he of the pet iguana and the fleet of roaches.

"Dude, your dog is running up and down Hanover Avenue."

Chad could taste metallic fear. The only way Chivas could be out was if someone had broken into his place. There wasn't anything worth stealing, but...his dog!

"Morris, go out and get him, he knows you, I'll be right there!" Chad threw a ten on the bar and ran towards Morris' place on Hanover. By the time he got there, he was out of breath but Chivas was happily rolling around in the grass outside Morris' apartment.

"I gave him a hotdog. He's happy as a clam."

The big black dog rolled over again and gave his friend a dog equivalent of a dopey grin.

"Great," Chad told Morris, "Now he'll hork *that* up all over the damned apartment."

"You said he's been acting weird lately. He seems fine to me."

"He's just not used to the new place yet. He'll calm down in a while. Listen, dude, will you come back with me to check the apartment? If someone's still in there, I don't want to meet him alone."

"Right, 'cause the chemistry geek is the one you want to back you up. Hang on, I gotta lock up."

They walked back to the Westchester. "When we get there," warned Chad, "we head right up. I don't want to run into the weird old lady downstairs."

Approaching the front of the apartment house, Chivas growled and whined. "What's wrong, buddy?" Chad asked the dog. "You just don't like this place, do you?" Entering, Chad was surprised to see that during the day there had been some renovation in progress. At least, someone had swept the leaves out and polished the mosaic floor. It really is nice, he thought. And a huge aquarium stood in one corner, a big tank on an ornate bronze stand. It was empty, though. Maybe someone had found it in the basement.

The men rushed upstairs to find Chad's door still locked.

"Jesus. They must have come in a window!" cried Morris.

"And Chivas jumped out from the second floor?" They moved inside. "There's just no way, dude. Why would anyone climb all that way up here? It's at least twenty feet. And Chivas would have hurt himself jumping out." They scanned the apartment. Every window—even the narrow bathroom window—was unbroken and tightly locked.

Morris was now beside himself. "This makes no sense, man," he said, "nobody's broken in here. How the hell did he get out?"

Chad had pretty much figured it out, he thought. "Dude, for a science guy, you have no logic. Did you see all that work they did in the lobby today? The landlords must be fixing the place up, or something. The maintenance guy must have come in and Chivas got out. I've been complaining about that damned toilet for a month now."

It pleased him that he might finally have a fully functioning apartment. Chivas, on the other hand, howled. Chad still felt bad for his dog, but it worried him all the same. If Chivas became too much of a nuisance, he could get kicked out of the apartment, which was really not what he needed right now. Sighing, he went to take a leak. The toilet still wouldn't flush.

After another week of classes, Chad had learned to cope with Willow and her particular brand of crazy. He found himself in a strange position: raised in the Washington suburbs, he wasn't used to feeling any sympathy for the rest of Virginia. Yet, here he was, confronted with a woman from Lynchburg - the very essence of Old Virginia - and defending Virginia itself against both Willow and Professor Ritter.

They found that their arguments tended to run in circles around a few points. Willow liked to point at the Capitol building as a "temple of the people," while Chad preferred the Jefferson Hotel, which Willow claimed was "a monument to capitalism and consumption." Chad tried to refrain from pointing out that her family, the aristocratic Virginian type if ever there was one, had done very well by profiting from capitalism and consumption. "If there were no wealthy people, how would anyone have ever built either the Jefferson or the Capitol? We're supposed to be thinking about important architecture, anyway. Should the whole town look like some kind of Soviet housing project?"

"No, but it looks too much like old Virginia elite. It was a classist, racist system."

"Of which you're a product, by the way. Besides, if we do away with stuff like the Jefferson, will that make everyone automatically equal?"

"People will never be truly equal until...."

"Eugenie, come to the Golden Heart Ball with me. Wear shoes, though."

And so it came to pass that the Establishment and the Counterculture went on their first date.

When Chad arrived at the Chesterfield apartments to pick up his date, the annoying artsy girl of last week—no, yesterday—had become the dictionary definition of a Southern belle. The straggling hippie hair had been arranged with tiny roses; the tie-dye replaced by an organdie gown and—Chad was pleased to note—she did have beautiful legs, and she was indeed wearing shoes.

There is no need to describe the Golden Heart Ball, or to describe the very clichéd circumstances in which a boy from yuppie Washington suburbia fell in love with a girl from Lynchburg. Let it suffice to say that the young lady that night ceased her insistence on calling herself "Willow," and that the young man became rather less intent upon Having It All.

They moved on the dance floor that night in a series of old dances that frustrated the young fraternity men, but which pleased the older alumni gathered there. Most of the undergraduate brothers preferred to sit these out, but Chad thought that Eugenie might like the waltzes, and she was certainly dressed for the part.

"You know, I judged you, Chad."

"You did. It was damned obvious. I judged you too, though."

"I know it. What did you think?"

"That you automatically hated me for being a fraternity man—am I right?"

"You are. I still think frat boys are assholes."

"I probably am, anyway. Do you at least think I'm a little smarter than I look, now?" She did not reply, but smiled at him as they danced on.

"Oh, Mr. Lennon!" The old woman called out from her apartment door.

"I hear you are doin' research on old Richmond buildings. Why don't you let me show you some of my ol' pictures?" Chad wasn't sure what to make of this; the old bat was undeniably creepy, but she also probably did know a lot about this stuff.

"I spoke with your friend already," she said. "Why don't you all join me for drinks real soon? I just love that you all are workin' on this kind of thing. Y'all are such nice young people, it's so nice to see y'all takin' an interest in the city like this!"

Chad walked up to his apartment. Thankfully, Chivas wasn't whining, for once. But the dog looked at him and acted like he was a stranger. He poured food into the dog's bowl, but Chivas wouldn't even come near him. This dog, Chad thought, is seriously losing it. He settled down for a night of studying.

The next morning proved to be a standard damp and drizzly Richmond winter day. On his way through the lobby (which was beginning to look quite good after all - someone had reconnected the gas logs in the fireplace and they cast a cheerful glow on the damp morning) he was accosted, inevitably, by Mrs. Mitchell. He decided to bite the bullet and told her that if it were alright, he and Eugenie would stop by that afternoon to look at photographs.

Meeting Eugenie for lunch, he brought up the proposed meeting with his neighbor. "I thought it would be OK with you, since you'd talked to her about it. She probably does have a bunch of good stuff we could use."

Eugenie looked at him blankly. "That sounds good, but...Chad, I've never talked to any of your neighbors." Chad realized that he'd just assumed his neighbor had meant Eugenie when she said "friend." Maybe she'd cornered Morris or someone. Still, it was weird; who else would really have known that much about this project?

By the time they got back to the Westchester, the dampness

had turned into actual rain. The gas fire in the lobby was now particularly welcome.

Mrs. Mitchell was, of course, waiting in her doorway. "Come on in, y'all, I have some tea and things waitin' for you."

Chad and Eugenie walked into the apartment. It had obviously been decorated nearly forty years earlier and hadn't been touched since. The living room furniture, the dining room, all of it was right out of a fifties Sears catalog. Waiting for them in the living room was a fully-set tea table. Chad wasn't quite sure what to make of all of this, but Eugenie felt right at home. He scrambled desperately to remember what little he knew about silver service and teacups, but Eugenie saved him by offering to pour the tea. She took charge of what must have been a priceless old teapot and served each of them, then picked up a little pair of silver tongs and distributed tiny sandwiches.

"Y'all young people now," said Mrs. Mitchell, "just don't know what the city was like. It was so beautiful years ago. Now, with all these old skyscrapers, it's just not the same. Now, what were y'all thinkin' about for your project?"

Chad mentioned the buildings they'd researched while Eugenie sat uncharacteristically quiet, drinking her tea.

Mrs. Mitchell procured a box of ancient postcards. Most of them were the same pictures they'd seen, though, buildings like the Academy and Murphy's. "I have just the place for you, Mr. Lennon," said the old lady, rifling the box to find something. "Oh, here we are. Have y'all heard of Pratt's Castle?"

They hadn't.

The pair began looking at the pictures that Mrs. Mitchell

handed them. It wasn't the biggest house Chad had ever seen, but it had to be one of the weirdest. It was undeniably majestic; the house really did look like a Gothic castle, with crenellated turrets and balconies, and a glass conservatory that overlooked the river. "Where *was* this thing?" Chad asked his hostess.

"Oh, it's not really gone," she replied. "I mean, it's not there now, but it saw an awful lot of Richmond's history, and it will always really be there. It's on Gamble's Hill." Confused by the weird answer, Chad pointed out that they had to work with a building that was actually demolished.

"Well, of course it doesn't really stand anymore," the old woman giggled, "but Pratt's Castle is never really going to be gone, I guess. Why, you know when it was torn down, some of the foundation stones were used to build the Westchester."

Eugenie looked over to Chad and said, "This is what we need." Chad wasn't sure, and Mrs. Mitchell was giving him the willies more than ever. He elected to silence himself in favor of the missionary glow that had appeared in his girlfriend's eyes.

Thelma Ritter found something subconsciously frightening about the proposal that one of her teams had submitted. She had, in fact, intended to use some of her undergrads' work as a stepping stone for herself. She did not like Richmond, with its self-satisfied air, its complacent surety of its own importance, its "and-who-are-you?" attitude. Nor did she particularly like either of these students. One represented that same snooty Virginia that she hated; the other was just an irritating fratboy business major. As a professor of social history, and a student of architecture, she was more than familiar with the old mansion that once had stood on Gamble's Hill, and she couldn't put her finger on why it bothered her that these two kids had lit upon it.

It was Christmas Eve when Chivas ran off for good. Chad had decided to stay in town for the holiday. Since his parents' fairly recent and very unpleasant divorce, Christmas didn't promise to be much fun at home. Besides, Eugenie had decided to stay in town as well.

On the morning of Christmas Eve, he was on his way out of the door when the dog yelped and tore past him. Before he'd even realized what happened, Chivas had run downstairs and out the front door, where another tenant whom he'd never met was bringing her groceries inside.

He spent the day searching the neighborhood, but his pet was nowhere. No hope lost, he thought; everyone in the neighborhood was crazy about animals and surely someone would take him in. He could find the dog soon. He had a date with Eugenie that night and surely Chivas would turn up by then.

A few days worth of serious effort with their project produced a good result. They were able to assemble a fairly comprehensive plan for the demolished building, and designed a presentation to accompany it. Chad and Eugenie celebrated with a few drinks at Bogart's. When Chad returned to the Westchester that December 30th, he could think of very little but the date he had for the night following. He had decided to take Eugenie to the Jefferson for dancing (partially to tease her for deriding that monument to capitalism). He decided to hang out in the lobby for a while, so, gathering a drink and a book, he settled into one of the big sofas. Mrs. Mitchell came out. How, he thought, does this woman always know when I'm here?

"I thought you might like some coffee," she said, putting a cup down before him and taking a seat. "I'm so pleased that you decided to work on Pratt's Castle after all. Here, you just warm up and read. You're gonna need all your strength, if you're going to dance the night away at the Hotel's New Years Ball."

Only the next morning did it occur to Chad that he'd never told anyone—even Eugenie—where he'd planned to take her that night.

Although his plan had been to hire a cab and take Eugenie right to the Jefferson, his neighbor clearly had something else in mind. Mrs. Mitchell caught him coming in, evening suit over one arm and a spray of flowers in the other.

"I do want y'all to call on me before you get down to the Hotel," she said.

Chad thought that she was acting more odd than usual, but she had helped them on that project. And, Eugenie seemed to like her.

When he got to the Chesterfield, he found Eugenie waiting in the lobby. He was stricken once again with her beauty. How could this delightful creature, in her white evening gown, be the same girl he'd met in Doc Martens and tie-dye four months earlier?

Lovely or not, she was clearly agitated. "Chad, the weirdest thing just happened. Professor Ritter came here an hour ago. I think she was wasted. She was a total mess; she told me that we had to stay away from Pratt's Castle."

He laughed. "She's right. We really shouldn't go near a house that was torn down fifty years ago."

"It freaked me out, Chad. She looked crazy. She told me that a big black dog warned her."

"Oh, hell. Everyone gets drunk on New Years Eve." The black dog reference was creepy, though, as Chivas hadn't turned up yet. "Let's go. Mrs. Mitchell wants to see us all dressed up for the party."

Returning to the Westchester a few minutes before eight, they were greeted by even more improvements to the building. The lobby was now augmented with a big Stieff grand piano and several more chairs.

It was full of people. Some seemed familiar, but Chad and Eugenie couldn't really place any of them. They were on their way to Mrs. Mitchell's door when she emerged.

Mrs. Mitchell had been transformed as surely as the room had been. Though an elderly woman, she glided out of the apartment as though she were still a debutante, geared up in a gown of lace laid over green taffeta. "Y'all are our guests tonight," she told the pair. "Take a glass of champagne."

Eugenie was not sure about this. She looked at Chad. "Oh, Mrs, Mitchell, this is lovely of you—but Chad made a reservation, we can't stay long."

"Oh, nonsense, sweetheart. I'll just ring down to the Hotel and tell them to hold your table there at the Empire Room." The woman seated at the piano looked up at the couple and smiled. She began to play a fox-trot: "It Had To Be You." The other party guests began to dance.

Chad whispered, "I don't know how to do this!"

"I do," Eugenie answered. "Just dance."

Immediately, other couples joined them to dance on the mosaic tiles. When the next song began someone cut in on him. It was Morris. "What the hell are you doing here?" he asked his fraternity brother.

"I don't know. I'm just here."

Chad found himself dancing with Mrs. Mitchell. He couldn't deny that she did dance very well. He recalled that years before, his grandfather had tried to teach him how to dance, telling him that "a woman likes a man who'll dance." Mrs. Mitchell could still dance as though she were much younger. Chad actually enjoyed dancing with the old woman, and was amused that she knew exactly what to do when one of the other party guests yelled out "Shake a wicked knee!"

The pianist ceased with the last notes of "Oriental Love Dreams." Mrs. Mitchell excused herself and, while Chad aimed for the punch bowl, Morris grabbed his arm. "Get out. Get out of here now. I don't want to be here and I don't know how the hell I got here. Take Eugenie and GO."

"Dude. You're wasted. It's cool, we're going downtown in a few. Just go over to Bogart's and chill."

"It's not cool. I'm supposed to be with my family out in Roanoke, but I'm not and I don't know why. GO." And then Morris was gone. He went to where Eugenie sat and took her arm.

"Let's go. This is getting weird." As they stood to make their farewells—after all, these folks had been very nice—Mrs. Mitchell called them aside.

"I know y'all are headed down to the Jefferson," she said, "but I thought you might have wanted a little party first. I'm glad y'all came. The work you did on that project was real important, and I want y'all to see somethin' else before you go downtown." Chad looked at his watch. It was almost ten, and he'd reserved a table for half past nine. "Y'all remember that I told you how the Westchester was built out of Pratt's Castle's stones? Well, now I'm gonna show y'all the Castle." She led the pair into her apartment. "Come on in, y'all should see the place. You'll be at your ball in no time." Chad and Eugenie looked at each other warily, but followed. They never heard the frantic pounding on the front doors of the Westchester Apartments.

Chad and Eugenie followed Mrs. Mitchell through the kitchen of her apartment, and into what seemed to be a wine cellar behind it. From there, they found themselves in a dim stone-walled hallway. And, soon, they were climbing an iron staircase, and emerged into a room blazing with light. "Here you are, y'all. Here is your bridal party." For there were at least fifty people there, and they knew that they were, in fact, inside Pratt's Castle. As the other party guests rose to greet them, Chad was separated from Eugenie, and shortly was ushered into a room full of other men. If he hadn't known better, he'd have imagined it to be a costume party, for beside him were men dressed in any number of strange outfits. To his left was a guy dressed like a fifties greaser. On the other side was a man in Confederate gray; and nearby was a man in Teddy Roosevelt-era evening clothes. Across the room was a man in twenties golfing attire.

He was now more than a bit confused, and more than a bit

apprehensive. "What in hell is going on here?" he asked the other men (who were all pointedly looking at him.)

The man in the freaky Jazz Age golf outfit answered. "My friend, you're the new groom. And your lovely friend in there is the new bride."

"Umm." Chad stuttered. "I don't think y'all quite get it. We're not... well, we are, but... I mean, we're not getting married."

The greaser looked at Chad. "Buddy, hate to say this, but you're the one don't get it. Hiram, maybe you oughta explain it. You were the first."

The Confederate sighed. "One more time, I guess. Well, friend, why don't you have a seat. Leroy, get our new friend a drink." The greaser went to a carved sideboard and poured whiskey. The Confederate sat near Chad. "Now, one thing most folks don't know is, Richmond ain't all that you see walkin' round town. It's a nice enough place, but underneath this town are some things that ain't real nice. An awful lot of awful bad things come real close to the surface here."

Chad laughed in disbelief. "Are you seriously saying that Richmond is the like the gate to Hell?"

"Maybe not the way you're thinkin'. But lemme tell ya, friend. This place is the closest that living folks can get to... well, I'm gonna say real bad things that they shouldn't oughta be close to."

The Jazz Age golfer spoke up again. "If it helps, I'll tell you that when people die, they pass damned close to Richmond, Virginia on their way to... wherever it is they're going."

"Ya see," the soldier went on, "Mr. Pratt was the first one to figure all that out. He built this house for his new bride, but she died right after they were married. It was when she was laid out for her funeral right here in this parlor when he realized how close you are to the other side when you're in Richmond. He realized that you needed something good and pure to keep all that bad mess where it is and where it belongs. And, he figured, ain't nothin' so good and pure as a happy bride and groom on their wedding day."

The greaser chimed in, "So ya see, buddy, he decided, right before he jumped off the tower of this house, that there should always be a bride and groom to watch over Richmond and keep it safe. But folks do get tired, and that's why you're here. There has to be a new honeymoon couple every once in a while. And I'm ready to retire. Ya see, I'm Leroy Mitchell. Y'all already met my wife Lorraine."

Mrs. Mitchell had been waiting for her cue, and now she walked in, no longer a batty old lady, but young and pretty. She was still wearing the taffeta dress, just as she had, Chad now understood, when she and Leroy had first blundered into Pratt's Castle. Leroy continued. "Ain't a bad time here, really. No way out of it, but you got this big ol' house and everything you're gonna need."

The gas lights of the Castle flared brighter, and Eugenie appeared in the door behind Lorraine Mitchell. The men in the room rose and opened the big chestnut doors that joined all of the Castle's rooms together. A band stationed in the hall began to play and struck up the "Belles of Richmond" waltz. Regarding each other in stunned silence, Chad and Eugenie began to dance.

The party over, the new bridal pair carefully climbed the

wrought-iron stairs that led to the turret of Pratt's Castle on Gamble's Hill. Below them to the south rumbled the great Falls of the James; surrounding them were the city's streets, sleeping peacefully on the other six hills. Holding hands, they surveyed their new domain.

News item:

Richmond, VA (AP): VCU Professor Is Apprehended in Bizarre Series of Events

Thelma Ritter, 48, was arrested by Richmond city police officers in the early hours of January 1. Security officers at a S. 4th street office building had contacted police, having noted the woman's erratic behavior. According to police, Ritter had been wandering the grounds of the corporate offices for several hours. She appeared disheveled and distraught. When approached, she began screaming at the officers, insisting that she "get to....Pratt's Castle."

"Pratt's Castle" was a nineteenth-century house, destroyed in 1946, that sat upon the land now occupied by the Ethyl Corporation. With Ritter was a large black dog, who was transferred to the Richmond SPCA, but which escaped shortly thereafter.

The Conjurer

Andrew Goethals

"There are things I will need from the Conjurers Society." The old man whispered. The basement was cold and musty, despite the thick heat of the Richmond summer. A bare light bulb hung from the ceiling, dark and covered with a film of dust, and the candle burning on the table left most of the room in darkness.

Angie shivered and wished she had worn a sweater. She watched the old man reach into the pocket of his coat, his fingers nothing but leathery skin stretched tight over bones, bent with arthritis. The old house above groaned, and she wet her lips nervously, looking up, wondering how long it took an abandoned building to collapse under the weight of years.

The man sitting across the table from her was as ancient as she had ever seen. He was gaunt and dry as a mummy, and his movements were nearly as stiff. He wore a black wool suit that hung off his shoulders as if he had shrunk inside it. His head was bare, except for a few wisps of white hair, and his eyes were hidden behind sunglasses. The scar tissue that marred his face suggested he might be blind, and the way his head moved from side to side seemed to confirm it for her.

The hand emerged from the coat, holding a sheet of lined paper, torn from a notebook and yellowed with time. As he unfolded it, little shreds of paper fell on the table, and the page nearly separated into quarters along the folds. The writing was elegant but archaic, and Angie wondered if this page was older than she was. It probably was, she realized; if this man was who he claimed, he had been banished from the Richmond Conjurers Society before she was born.

She had first heard the name of Peter Czerny twenty years ago, sitting at another table. She had been sitting at a booth at Millie's on a Sunday morning, holding her coffee with both hands and waiting for the harried waitress to bring her eggs. It was winter, and they had been seated too near the door, so the cold air slipped over her shoulder and along her spine each time the door opened, and still the line stretched around the corner. Her eye went from the window to the mug in her hand, but not to the man across from her.

He was old enough to be her grandfather, and had that mothballed, tweedy look. His beard was white and the lines between his brow were etched deep from years of heavy thinking. He was the most brilliant Conjurer in the Society, who had bound spirits and questioned them for days. She was only a novice, still in her first year of study, and had been honored by his interest. He had been generous with his knowledge and she had drunk every drop, and asked for more.

"Such beautiful lips," he had said, when they were in the small apartment he kept.

"What do you mean?" She was a thick, awkward girl who had spent her youth hidden in books, studying arts so obscure that most of the world did not believe in them. She had never been wanted before. When he kissed her, she was stunned. She had endured much in her short life. She had crossed wits with demons, but to kisses she had no defense. It was more amazing to her than any spirit summoned from outside the universe.

The next morning, at Millie's in the same clothes that he had taken off of her the night before, she was still stunned, and as the old man rationalized, she hardly listened.

"...not as bad as what Czerny did," he was saying, "but still, if anyone found out..."

"Czerny?" she interrupted. "What did he do?"

"Peter Czerny," he said, grateful to have something to talk about besides why what had happened between them could not happen again. "He tried to corporealize a spirit. To give it a physical body. This would have been, oh, twenty years ago, I think. He was a genius, but never understood that there are reasons..."

The waitress set their plates down, and asked if there was anything else. Angie never touched her food, though, and she lost interest in Peter Czerny. She had finally realized that she was being discarded by the first man who had ever wanted her.

"Taking these will get me banned," she said. She slid the list back across the table. Peter Czerny bared his ancient, yellowed teeth, and his shoulders shook. It took Angie a moment to realize he was laughing at her, but there was no mistaking the mocking sneer that twisted his withered lips.

"Only if they know it was you who took them. If the guardian spirits saw another enter, there would be no reason to suspect you, would there?" His speech was a breathy rattle, and every few syllables he paused to inhale. Even that brief speech seemed to exhaust him, and he slumped back in his chair. "You could lend me your key."

She reached down to lift the key that she wore on a chain around her neck. It was silver, and it unlocked almost all of the doors in the Conjurers Society hall. Only the Master had the gold key, but Peter would be able to get the things that were on his list with the silver.

"Can you really corporealize a spirit?" she asked. "It is supposed to be impossible."

"Now why would they ban me for attempting something impossible?" he asked.

"Is it true?" she asked again.

Instead of answering, he simply held up a hand and beckoned. Angie gasped, as a shape moved out of the shadows to stand behind him, but once it moved into the light, she shook her head. It was a girl in a hooded sweatshirt, with a thick cotton veil over her face.

"What is that?" Angie said. "A woman in a hoodie?"

Peter reached back and rested a hand on the girl's wrist, pulling the hand free of the pocket and into the candle light. A graceful, feminine hand with skin so pale and delicately smooth that it might never have felt the sun's touch rested gently in his twisted claw. Even the blue lines of the veins under her skin seemed elegant, and Angie felt the bitter taste of jealousy that she so often felt when she faced beauty, just from the sight of the hand.

"Pull back your hood, dear," Peter rasped.

The perfect hand pulled the hood away slowly, revealing two beautiful, sky blue eyes that glistened like clean spring sun in the dank, musty cellar. The forehead was as pure and smooth and pale as the skin of her hand, and her hair was the ripe gold of summer wheat. Angie stared at her in awe, as she tucked her hair behind her ear.

"And the veil."

The sparkling azure eyes turned to the elderly wizard, who could not return their gaze, but a grin stretched his mouth and revealed his crooked teeth. He nodded, and the creature beside him reached up to lower the veil. Her nose was long and graceful and her cheeks delicate and high. Below her nose, though, the flesh lost its delicate pallor and showed plain white like wax. Weird lumps added to the impression, as though her face had melted, and there was no chin or lower jaw to speak of, just bulbous globs of something horrible and flesh-like.

Worse than any of that was the mouth, if that word could even be used. Below her nose was an opening, round and surrounded with narrow white tendrils that writhed like so many fat maggots, reaching out towards Angie and curling back, as if beckoning to her. The thing's eyes rolled back and there was a gurgling sound from that disgusting hole.

The old man chuckled and wheezed. "She likes you. Do you want to kiss her?"

Angie retched and had to clench her teeth to keep from losing her supper over the table. Her mouth filled with the acid taste of bile, a taste that seemed clean by comparison to the idea of feeling those hideous feelers touching her lips. She turned away and heaved in the corner, the contents of her stomach splattering horribly onto mildewed straw. When she turned back, the veil was back in place, and the old man held the creature's hand tenderly.

"Do you believe now?" he asked.

She was nearly thirty before she found her first clue about where Czerny had gone after he was banned from the Conjurers Society. She had her brass key, then, and had begun working major bindings. It had been a brisk day in January when the creature she had summoned asked her to make it a body.

"It can't be done," she said. "Possessions cause the death of both the spirit and the host." It was elementary, lead key stuff, that every neophyte conjurer learned. Those that didn't, usually ended up allowing a spirit into their body and dying as a result.

"Said make me a body. Like Black Peter did for Anabel, by the round rock."

Days of digging through the Society's records led to no mention of any Black Peter or Peter Black. The binding she had put on the imp made it impossible for the creature to lie to her without suffering terrible agonies, but it was well known that the spirits went to great lengths to mislead, without actually telling lies.

As soon as she began to look for records of attempts at corporealization, she came across Peter Czerny's name, and it did not take long for her to learn that black in Polish, is Czerny. It wasn't long after that that she learned that Peter had come from

Poland in the late 1930s, and that the crime he had been banished for was his attempt to create a body for a spirit to inhabit.

Finding the round rock took her another two years, but her instinct was right in that case. The river rocks were all round, and on an island on the south shore, just below the Boulevard Bridge, she found the circle Peter had drawn decades before. The bones she found nearby led her to suspect that the brilliant conjurer had attempted to guide a spirit safely into a host body, but it had rebelled.

She had learned to summon the spirits of the deceased before she had even heard of the Conjurers Society.

"The girl by the round rock?" she asked.

"She was the beginning," the ancient man said. "The poor dear thought I was going to teach her to summon spirits. It was a pity, she had the most beautiful blue eyes, but I had promised Anabel a body."

Angie looked at the grotesque creature behind him, her knees still trembling and her stomach still churning. The thing behind the man had no expression in its perfect blue eyes, as it looked at her, and Angie didn't try to meet its eye or conceal her revulsion.

"You came here to learn, I believe?"

Angie nodded her head. The hideous creature turned and vanished back into the shadowy recesses of the cellar, returning with a stack of notebooks. It set them on the table by the old man.

"My research notes. I have performed the rituals enough that I no longer need them. Besides," he gestured towards his sunglasses and the scars they only partially hid. "I can no longer read them."

Angie reached across the table slowly, but the thing leaned forward, and she heard that horrible, gurgling hiss coming from its mouth again. She pulled her hand into her lap and shrank back in her chair. The old man patted his monster's hand gently, almost tenderly.

"She may read them," he said, head tilted back towards the thing. "For one hour. Then she must give us her key."

It kept its beautiful blue eyes on Angie, but stepped back. Away from the candle in the dusty shadows, it could almost pass for a woman. Angie took the top notebook, and opened it slowly, the pages stiff and brittle with age and the ink faded. The handwriting was tight and jerky, and she had to lean close to the pages to read it, but it was pure brilliance. She looked up at the old man and smiled, her perfect teeth framed beautifully by her soft lips.

Her smile had always been the one thing about her that was beautiful. Peter grinned at her from his near skeletal face, and nodded encouragingly. The cold air seemed to wrap around her as she read of his first experiments with flesh and blood, when he was still at the Conjurers Society.

After the first bones by the James, Angie began to search harder. She hired a detective to try to find Peter Czerny in the mundane world, but she had little hope for his success. Conjurers tended to live out of sight of the rest of humanity, and they tended to cling to the old. The Richmond Conjurers Society had been known as the Royal Conjurers Society of Richmond until the very early twentieth century, and only the youngest members lived in places with electric lights. She was the only one she knew of who had so much as an email address.

As she expected, the investigator had little luck. She had better luck, talking to demons and imps, ghosts and sprites that she bound in her summoning circles. Apparently, Black Peter was quite well known in the world beyond the world, and all the creatures she spoke to asked for bodies now.

The process was desperately slow. The creatures of the outer world only could glimpse him when he performed magic, but they spoke of what he was doing with awe. Each glimpse showed the body he was making growing, each clue sent Angie searching for some other half-seen location. A twisted tree, a stone obelisk, a bronze horse. Over the course of six years she found three more sites where Peter had drawn his circles and sacrificed a life to give a spirit from beyond a true body of its own.

At times, she would think of the horror of sacrificing human lives for such a thing. Like most conjurers, though, humanity had not been kind to Angie. She had spent most of her life trying not to be noticed, because she had learned early on that she was different. She had learned how cruel humanity could be, and when she really thought about it, there were plenty of people she would gladly sacrifice to create a new life. A better life.

It was in the seventh year that she got the email. Just a short note. "I understand you've been looking for me. Peter Czerny." That, and a time and date, and the address of this crumbling old house on Oregon Hill. It had seemed too good to be true, but she never thought for a moment of not going. The man had vanished before she was born, and had left virtually no trace, but he had contacted her.

For the second time in her thirty seven years, a man had chosen her. When she got to the house, she hardly noticed the boarded up windows and the crumbling brickwork. She waded through the jungle that the yard had become to the cellar door at the back of the house, and she went in, down the creaking steps into the cold dark cellar, where an old, blind man sat waiting for her with a single candle burning.

"There are things I will need from the Conjurers Society," he said when she had sat in the chair opposite him. In the darkness, she had never seen the twisted summoning circle drawn on the floor.

She had to restrain herself from tearing through the pages. They were old enough that they would tear, and the mind revealed by the writings was astounding to her. The ideas were absolutely revolutionary, going against centuries of tradition, but at the same time, they made perfect sense. She read some paragraphs twice, or three times, in order to understand exactly what he meant.

She looked at the stack of notebooks. She was only looking at the oldest, the first steps on the path. She could hardly imagine what else she might discover. She felt a little shiver and brought her attention back to the page.

"Tea?" the old man said, most politely. "You would not want to take a chill."

"Thank you," she murmured, without lifting her eye from the page. It seemed only a moment before the creature he called Anabel set a steaming mug down on the table beside her.

She turned another page and took a sip. It had a strange

sweetness to it, but she felt the warmth of it spreading through her. She stared at the page in front of her and heard the old man murmuring. There were words, words that seemed so familiar to her, if only she could remember what they meant.

She looked up at the creature, and saw that hideous hole, heard it gurgling as though from far away. As the drug in the tea pulled her into darkness, she saw the thing leaning down, until the hole and the writhing tendrils of flesh around it was the only thing she could see.

Then that was gone too.

Anabel shuddered with pleasure as she straightened, fingers touching her soft, glistening lips, tracing the shape of her graceful jaw, the skin as delicate and beautiful as the rest of her body. She smiled and her perfect white teeth seemed to shine.

The girl from the Conjurers Society was dead, lying across the table in a drying pool of her own blood, her face horribly mutilated, and the old man chanted slowly, finishing the incantation for the last time. He reached up with his withered fingers to touch her chin, her neck, the silken skin more perfect than any human's, and he smiled.

"At last," he whispered.

"At last," she echoed, surprised as the warmth of her new voice, amused by the strange feeling of making words. It would take practice. It didn't matter, though. After forty years and more murders than she could remember, she was finally whole, her body perfect and beautiful, far better than merely human.

"My creation," he whispered, and slowly lifted his feeble body out of his chair. He had kept himself alive long years beyond his normal life span to finish creating her. For years, she had been trapped in an incomplete body, denied the familiarity of her home beyond the world, but unable to function as a human. For decades, she had been his shadow, watching and waiting for him to find suitable girls, pretty and mystically aware, baited with curiosity, and then murdered for their flesh. She knew how it was done. She pulled the sweatshirt over her head and dropped it to the floor, looking down at her body, stolen from dozens of innocents.

"You're perfect," he whispered.

"Perfect," she echoed.

"You're mine," he cackled, and reached for a perfectly rounded breast.

She looked down at his ancient, withered body and took him in her arms.

He began to laugh, but it cut off suddenly as she gave his head a sharp twist and snapped his neck. She had been patient, letting him use her, in her prison of unfinished flesh. She was complete now, and perfect, and would not let the withered old thing use her any longer. She took the key from around the dead girl's neck. She was perfect, and she would have a perfect mate.

There were things she would need from the Conjurers Society.

The Bike Chain of Fate

Eric Hill

The bike messengers of Richmond are something like a modern Pony Express, a culturally fascinating but almost useless form of sending a message or a package a few miles away as quickly as possible. There was something quintessential about living in River City, when, expecting a delivery from your outer branch office, instead of meeting a pleasant man in a brown uniform you were greeted by an extremely sweaty guy in shorts, his beard dripping juice onto the tile. He would, after spitting in the soil of the fake office plants, smelling of bean sprouts and tobacco, lovingly hand you a stack of documents that, for some reason, were too expensive to mail.

It was from one of these bike messengers that I gained a brief insight into the interior mold of this strange tribe of men and women. I witnessed a bit of what they aspired to, I found out their great fear and, shortly thereafter, I suspended my doubts about the supernatural. I can't tell if these stories are true, but I can tell you that they kept me up at night. Watching those quickly rolling shadows outside of the windows of my house in the Fan, I began to wonder what sacred laws might apply to me. Can one group of men be bound by a supernatural law that others are not? What really happens after something crosses into the afterlife? Who is to say when something is alive or dead, but our own sense of reality?

This knowledge was passed to me in an elevator while working late one evening after a bike messenger had dropped off a series of nameplates from a local sign maker. We were putting new names on the doors of the offices of my law firm, and the shipping costs were too great to bother with for sending them only 5 miles, so we had the Radical Riders deliver the new nameplates.

Johnny Pickwickle, a small grungy kid with a red face and a dirty thick-striped shirt, took my signature and left my office like I had the plague. The messengers didn't like my kind, they had a thing against washing and capitalism, so they rarely stayed long and almost never spoke. By the time he closed the door I was looking in the brown package to check the order when I realized that one of the plates was missing. Not wanting to have to tip him to come back a second time I dashed down to the elevator to try and catch him before he took off.

I stopped Johnny in the elevator, just before the door shut. For some reason, which I still question today, he did not feel compelled to step out of the elevator when he saw me running. So instead I stepped in, and the door closed behind me. I was relieved to find that Johnny had only left the nameplate in his side bag, and after a "see you later dude" I turned about face to open the elevator door. To my dismay, it was stuck fast.

After pushing all of the buttons twice, trying the elevator phone and attempting to pry the door open, I realized that the power had cut out in the summer heat, and that in all likelihood, we would be trapped in the elevator until power was restored. As it turned out we were the last two people left in the building and we were trapped for the rest of the night. After standing for about twenty minutes, as if the situation would be improved by our posture, Johnny and I both sat down dismayed.

"I really hope my bike doesn't get snagged," said Johnny, who was playing with a red checkered bandana on his leg. He had a troubled look on his face, and kept rubbing his hand through his hair anxiously.

"How can you be worried about your bike when you're trapped in an elevator?" I asked, more angrily than I should have. Johnny smelled like rotted bananas and, being a biker, found it fashionable not to have a cell phone. I had left my Blackberry in the office. Johnny turned and spoke, his voice carrying a subtle tremor.

"My bike is my life, I mean what are you worried about, your 401 K?" replied Johnny with a mocking grin. This was early 2008 so I did not yet know how right he was. I wanted to punch him in his little pockmarked chin, but Johnny had a water bottle and several granola bars which I was hoping he would share with me, so I held back my judgment and fantasized about a potential lawsuit against the building manager. After a few minutes, and the sharing of the food and water Johnny spoke up again.

"Well, there is another reason I don't want to leave my bike, but you'll probably lose respect for me as a man." I didn't think I could lose something I didn't have, so I said I wouldn't and that I valued hardworking young men such as him.

"I'm afraid of being cursed," said Johnny. I immediately lost all respect for him as a human being.

"What are you talking about?" I said, as I chewed one of Johnny's homemade granola bars, which was surprisingly delicious and naturally organic.

"Amongst the most dedicated of all bikers, there is a bond between man and bike which can never be violated," said Johnny as serious as a heart attack, "It is called the bike chain of fate, and those who break it are doomed to die." Johnny spoke slowly and deliberately. The emergency elevator light flickered on and off for dramatic effect, like a high school drama class production.

"Why would you believe in a silly curse like that? It's ridiculous, thinking your bike has a bond with you. It's just a hunk of metal."

"What would happen if I keyed your Jag?" Replied Johnny, who somehow knew I had a Jaguar. "You don't know man, you really don't know," said Johnny, shaking his head, "this bike and I are like one. When we ride together she is my lover. If she was stolen it would be like adultery." Awed by this strange loyalty to his bike, I asked Johnny where he had heard of this curse.

"I've seen the curse unfold before - three times," he held out three greasy fingers and wiggled them like a shaman, "It is well known among my people. Every time a great rider dishonored his bike, they were brutally killed in a freak accident. Some say, it is because the bike takes its vengeance."

I snorted so hard when he said this that a bit of granola became lodged in my sinus. "I'd heard you biker kids were crazy, but this is a bit more than I can take."

"It's true!" said Johnny sticking his arms into the air like he was doing a pull-up, " Every time you see one of those bike skeletons chained to a Stop sign, there is a biker in his grave somewhere." Being that we were trapped in an elevator, and there were few options to pass the time, I consented and asked Johnny to tell me his stories.

"The first time I knew that there was something to the bike chain of fate, I questioned it. The gang and I were riding one day down Grace Street getting ready for a show. The band was called Painted Ladies. It was an all girl hardcore band playing down at Strange Matter. We were a little drunk, you know a few PBR's before we headed down there, and Petey forgot his bike lock.

"Normally we'd be like, fuck that, and we'd just chain the two bikes together and lock them somewhere, but we could not find a single spot outside. The Painted Ladies were popular, and the show was going to start in like, five minutes. Sure, we could have walked down the blocks looking for a spot, but Petey said 'forget it man, it's all wabi sabi.

"Petey didn't want to just leave his bike outside, so he thought he could just throw it in the dumpster behind the 7-11 until the show was over. This was definitely not wabi sabi. Petey had that bike for 7 years, and once you've gone 7 years with a bike, it's like your child. Would you leave your child in a dumpster?"

"Wait, I thought you said your bike was like your lover?" I interrupted.

"Does it make any difference?" I didn't want to say. Johnny gave me a stare that made me feel a little monstrous for thinking I could throw a girlfriend in a dumpster if I was drunk enough. After a few seconds of awkward silence, Johnny continued.

"So Petey, the gang and I go inside. We enjoy the show, drink a bit more and the drummer chick from Painted Ladies wants to go back to her friend's pad with Petey. By this time all of the rest of the gang had found our respective girls and were ready to go home. Had we been better bike mates, we would've remembered to get Pete's bike, but there was too much going on that night, so we ditched Petey and he went home with that chick."

"The next morning Petey remembered his forgotten bike and ran back to 7-11 to retrieve it. Well of course it wasn't there, every hobo in town goes through that dumpster every Saturday looking for leftover sandwiches, and the bike might not have been edible but it was certainly sellable. Forlorn, Petey went back to his house, and began to drink like a fish. The last time I saw Petey alive was Sunday, buried in beer cans, crying for Cecilia - that was his bike's name."

"Next Tuesday they found Petey in the Richmond city dump, his arms wrapped around Cecilia's tireless body. Her tires and Petey's shoes had been removed, both of them lying next to his corpse, as neatly as if they had been laid in front of his bed."

"Let me stop you right there," I said. I was a lawyer after all, and I had spoken to defense attorneys who saw this stuff all of the time.

"What's to say that Petey didn't go searching for his bike, got attacked by the person who found it, and then got dumped along with the evidence?"

"Well, sure, that's what everybody, including the gang and the police thought. Maybe he got a lump on the head and died," said Johnny wistfully, "though they ain't never found his killer and the crew still looks out for anyone who knows about Petey's death. Though once it happened I began to think about another time when mysterious events of this sort occured.

"It was the year before Petey's death, before we had really

gotten the gang started. Me, Petey, a girl named Debra and her boyfriend Fisher would regularly go biking along the James River and down near Pony Pasture. It was a warm July night, right before the Fouth, when Debra managed to score some magic mushrooms for us. We decided we were going to trip out on this little beach by the James and watch fireworks.

"It was a gorgeous night, we'd just come from the 821 Café and we took the mushrooms right before starting our long ride. Well, the best way to get to this beach is through Hollywood Cemetery, so we rode our bikes into the cemetery and shimmied down a cliff by the James. There's a lesson here, never trip mushrooms while trying to guide a bike down a cliff. Debra thought her bike was "really soft" so she decided to just fling it off the cliff, rather than putting it on her shoulder and carrying it down. Debra did not respect her bike. Debra had been riding Tony Danza for almost 9 years, and only 3 years ago Tony Danza had saved Debra's life when she had been hit by a speeding car. If Tony Danza had not been made out of high grade carbon fiber, Debra would have died.

"Naturally the cliff path was only a few feet from the river, so when Debra threw her bike it landed in the water, which was very high that night. The bike was light enough to be carried, and the powerful James swept up Tony Danza and swallowed him whole. Debra was too high to care. She shrugged it off and continued to trip with us as we went to the little beach.

"After a night of playing in the trees, talking nonsense and running around naked, the four of us passed out in a heap on the beach. Late that night, I had to take a piss, so I got up and went to the river. In the bright moonlight, as I took a mighty leak, I looked over the James and scanned downriver. Just beyond the bend where I could see, I witnessed one of the scariest sights a biker could possibly imagine. It was Tony Danza, pedaling himself up the river like a poly carbon Jesus.

"I hurried up with my leak and woke everybody up to show them the ghost bike, but once everyone was up and we looked back down river, Tony Danza was gone. Debra was kind of panicky, at this point she knew of the bond she'd had with her bicycle and she wanted to repent for her disrespect. Debra and Fisher decided they would go back to the cemetery cliff and try to find Tony Danza, to see if he might have washed up on shore somewhere. They looked all night and the next day, but they never found him. I chalked it up to the mushrooms, but I'd always have my doubts.

"A few days later, Debra drowned in the James. The police report said that she had several broken bones, which looked as if she had fallen from a height. Fisher was considered a suspect, but he was eventually cleared because he had an alibi working at the record store. The cause of death was eventually ruled as an accidental fall. They found Tony Danza, hanging by his wheel on a train bridge, miles up river from Hollywood Cemetery."

"It sounds like your friends all did too many drugs, and then suffered from accidents," I said, yawning as drowsiness began to set in. While I was getting tired it seemed as if Johnny was tweaking, his eyes bulged and his mouth frothed in its corners.

"Man I am thirsty," said Johnny. After a drink his nerves began to settle, and he looked me dead in the eyes and told me the third time he had witnessed the bike chain of fate.

"I could believe that Debra had accidentally drowned trying to reach Tony Danza. I could admit that maybe Petey went dumpster diving to find Cecilia and got caught in a compactor or something. It was shortly after Slaughterama though, that I knew for certain that the curse was real. I could try to explain to you what Slaughterama is, but you would probably think I was madman. It is a ceremony. It is an act of worship and daring. It is the immolation of a biker's soul, where he proves his salt by attempting great feats of bicycle derring-do." Johnny sounded like a radio announcer blended with a romance novelist when he talked about bicycles.

"Roberto Curtis was probably the best stunt cyclist in the Cutthroats bike gang, and that's a real compliment. Only the greatest of cyclists aspired to join the Richmond Cutthroats, and you had to really bleed to get that jacket patch.

"Roberto had many bikes, but there was one bike which he was very well known for, named Pure Evil. Pure Evil had been forged by Roberto's own hands, Roberto's blood had apparently been poured into the steel that made its frame, and mixed into the paint he used. The handle bars were actually the handles used to carry his mother's coffin. On those sacred handlebars were tassels made from his hair. Legends say Roberto once beat a man to death when he tried to steal Pure Evil, and supposedly that's where he got the human skin that covered his bicycle seat. Pure Evil was as much an extension of Roberto's body as his right arm.

"I was sitting at the base of the high jump ramp, watching the amazing stunts as cyclists were hoisted 20 feet into the air by their pedaling fury. It was here that I would witness Pure Evil murder a man. You see, the bike chain of fate isn't just a bond that exists between biker and bike. No, if another biker violates the chain of fate, then he will perish by the curse as well.

"A rider by the name of Gary took Pure Evil without Roberto's blessing. It was a stupid thing to do, because had Roberto found him, he would have done the deed himself. Gary lined up Pure Evil for a high jump with a front wheel twist. It was a pretty easy trick, and Gary was an experienced rider. I'd seen him before, there was no question he was good.

"Gary pedaled hard up to the ramp, he was going fast, fast enough to get 20 feet of air easily, but Pure Evil had other plans. Outside of the hands of his master, Pure Evil had a will of his own, and he was a nasty son-of-a-bitch. As the bike hit the ramp I could see the wheels moving, moving even though Gary wasn't pedaling, moving even though it was a fixed gear stunt bike. Gary flew 45 feet into the air, an impossible height for that ramp. When Gary reached the peak of his jump, he knew he was going to die. Pure Evil twisted in the air and flipped upside down; not backwards but forwards. When Gary hit the ground he broke his neck, but Pure Evil landed on both of his wheels. Then, and I shit you not, Pure Evil wheeled itself back to Roberto like a dog being called by its owner."

I didn't believe Johnny's stories for one minute, but I had to admit he could spin a damn good yarn, especially since he was probably trashed out of his pimply skull every time he saw this "bike chain of fate." Shortly after Johnny finished his stories I rolled over and went to sleep. In the night I could hear him, twisting and turning and whispering and farting. He was worried about something, he kept mumbling in a worried voice in his dreams.

After sleeping in the elevator for a few hours the maintenance man came and was able to open the door for us. As I walked out onto the first floor of the James Center, Johnny sprinted onto Cary Street. I saw him looking desperately up and down the street screaming out "Delilah!!!" I laughed a little bit at this, and in a better mood than I thought I would be in, I went home.

The next time I saw a bike messenger was six weeks later. I was waiting for a laptop that had just been repaired, when a sweaty, fat guy in bike shorts lumbered in with it. I asked him how a biker could get to be so big boned and he said, "Beer is my life force." The fat biker didn't leave immediately, so I figured he was holding out for a tip.

I pulled out a 5 dollar bill but before I gave it to him I asked, "Hey, you know that other bike messenger, Johnny, right?"

"Yeah, I used to know the Pickle, if that's what you mean," said the fat biker, a frown growing across his face.

"What do you mean?"

"Johnny was shot by some guy in Shockoe Bottom. He died just a couple blocks from here. It was all over the news." I handed the fat biker the five bucks and he left.

I went to my computer and looked up the demise of Johnny Pickwickle. Sure enough he had died almost six weeks ago, the day after we had met in the elevator. The death was still under investigation, but apparently the killer had left a note. On a sheet of tattered cardboard, covered in black bike tracks and written in blood was a message that read, "For Delilah."

I cannot say if voodoo will exist in a world run by machines and modern men, but if we are judged by the things we believe, then, maybe it won't matter. Perhaps it will take some other form, a form where our spirits live in the machines, and they have the will to follow us wherever we carry them. I did not know Johnny Pickwickle well, but he believed in a sacred bond, and a force that would reckon with those who violated it.

These days when I drive my Jaguar home, I can see them on their iron gazelles, coming out into the night. Their chains twirl and reflect the beam of my headlights, their legs pump up and down like throbbing ventricles. In the darkness I cannot say where their parts conjoin. Perhaps the Pickle was right, and for the true biker, man and cycle are one.

Everything Must Go

Melissa Scott Sinclair

Already the men's restroom stinks of coffee piss and desperation.

It's not even nine-fifteen.

I push through the door into the fourth-floor hallway of DR3. I know it's the fourth floor because the carpet by the elevators is pale green. I know it's DR3 because the carpet everywhere else is a footworn gray, and the cube walls are a nubbly gray, and the grout between the gray bathroom tiles is a gray filthy beyond the hope of Clorox.

DR3 is an enormous hive of concrete and glass. In its little gray cells squirm customer service reps, fraud investigators, web designers and production managers. And me, a proud product writer. I write stirring elegies to off-brand breadmakers.

There is no DR2.

DR1 is another block of concrete and glass where execs spend their days discussing strategic value propositions. In DR1 the lobby is polished granite and the carpet is fresh. The cubes are exciting shades of red and pale blue, arranged on the diagonal to enable cross-functional teamwork.

I'm happy I don't work in DR1. But I'd be happier if I didn't work at Circuit City at all. I've got my resignation letter printed, as a matter of fact. Just got to sign it. Just got to hand it in. Which I plan on doing soon—right after this pay cycle ends. Or the one after.

I should be gone already. This place is going the way of Betamax and DivX. Everyone knows that. And it would make my life a whole fucking lot simpler if I left, I tell you that. Ever since I hooked up with that admin—whatshername? Mallory—at the fourth-floor Christmas party, things have been bad. Like, look-around-corners bad.

I should be gone already. But I'm a contractor. I have no ties. I'm not one of the poor assholes who have company stock and 20-year Lucite trophies on their desks. I'm just along for the ride.

On the way back to my cube I nod to Boatshoes, a morning shitter so brazen he tucks his home-theater accessory catalogs under his arm to read in the men's room. Boatshoes doesn't notice. He almost runs me over on his way in—and just as abruptly, comes back out.

"Hey man," I say.

He only looks frantically down the corridor and then dashes off toward Waxlip's office.

I stand and watch, because this is weird. Boatshoes races back with Waxlip in tow. Waxlip is wearing his Deeply Concerned look, which means this has to be something really big. Last round of layoffs he wore Couldn't Be Helped. He usually saves Deeply Concerned for quarterly earnings reports.

They go together into the men's room. I follow them.

A man's lying on the tile, face to the urinals. He doesn't look relaxed, like he just passed out. He looks broken. A thin red pool creeps from under his sandy hair. It looks like an unrolled Fruit Roll-Up. It seeps into the collar of his pink button-down.

"Call 911," Waxlip orders. "And security." Boatshoes fumbles with his cell.

A little crowd gathers, women and men pressing into the fetid restroom. No one pounds the guy's chest. No one fastens their mouth on his, no one forces in a lungful of piss-smelling air. No one even touches him. They only stare, solemn and awkward and curious.

"He was a really nice guy," some woman says.

I don't want to know who it is. I feel sick. I push my way out of the men's room and follow the footworn carpet back to my gray box.

The whole day I can't get any work done. I stare so long at the CMS screen that it logs me out. I don't bother signing back in. Around me I hear people whispering about the poor guy. Did you see it? The poor guy.

I hear one of the programmers in the aisle, rounding up people to go to Chipotle. He skips my cube. I don't care. I don't feel like eating lunch anyway.

At 3:43, I can't take it anymore. I sneak down the gray carpeted stairwell to the side door. I pull my ID from the lanyard clipped to my pants and hold it up to the scanner.

No beep. Light stays red.

I swipe it, wave it, press it up to the slotted black box. Nothing. I walk down the hall to the main lobby. No one's there, which is weird. The desk where the sour old security guard sits is empty.

I push on the big glass front door and it doesn't even creak. The one next to it is locked too. It's dark outside. There are fifteen cars in the whole white-striped lot.

It shouldn't be night. It's June. Happy hour hasn't even started at Cap Ale.

I bang my fists on the glass. It doesn't quiver.

"Hey," I shout. No one comes.

I pull my cell from my pants pocket. Dead.

That's when I see the red stain spreading on my J. Crew shirt.

The first week I go mad.

I let the elevator doors crush my chest. Batter my head against the conference-room windows. Throw myself from the fourth-floor terrace in the fountained atrium of DR1. But it's like playing darts with a feather. I waft gently back and fall to the gray carpeted floor.

The second week I sit in my cube.

It feels safe. I think maybe I'll close my eyes and when I open them I'll be—I'll be here again. Nope. All I see is people stealing stupid shit from my desk. Boatshoes takes my Boba Fett bobblehead. I never really wanted it anyway; it was a freebie some vendor handed out. But still.

My ergonomic mousepad. My USB-powered fan. My signed Slipknot poster. I watch Burgs, my old Xbox buddy, cruise into my cube. He stares at the gray carpet for a minute. His mouth moves like he's saying a prayer. Then he reaches down and yanks the cord of my iPod dock from the wall.

"I see you, asshole," I say.

I think about the morning I walked up the steps of DR3 and saw a pigeon lying limp before the door. It had crashed into the glass, fooled by the mirrored sky.

I stood and looked at it. Bright blood pooled on the slate. Heels clicked by its shattered skull. Click click click. Finally a maintenance guy came and cleaned it up.

I've been cleaned up. There's not a trace of me on the gray tile in the men's room. By Friday, there's nothing left on my desk but an old PC, a stack of papers and an empty stapler. I'm not even good gossip anymore. Aneurysm was the word I heard over the cube walls. Aneurysm. It sounds gross, something for old people. It's not fair. It's not fair at all. I'm not even 30.

The third week, I think. I think hard. I'm a smart guy. I can get out of here.

I do the logical thing: I try all the doors. The side doors, the emergency exits, the mailroom. I get lucky in the first-floor cafeteria, with the door that leads to the grassy courtyard between DR1 and DR3. I slip out in the backdraft of two accountants, white Marlboro Lights already perched between their fingers.

I make it. I'm Out. I'm standing on the sidewalk, squinting in the sun.

Across the courtyard and through a strip of woods there's the side parking lot. I wonder if my Camry's still there, the windshield hazed with pollen. Suddenly I want to see it more than anything. I want my car, my shitty sensible sedan with Starbucks stains on the seats. I want it so bad.

I wonder if the keys jangling in my phantom pocket might just work.

I follow the accountants down the butt-littered path that curves into the trees. It's strange, being outside. I don't like it. But I have to get to my car.

The sun makes me drunk. The asphalt wavers. It sucks at my feet. It laps like a tongue.

Sssssss.

There in front of me are geese. A whole flock of hissing geese, the same fat-ass birds that shit little green logs all over the parking lot. They stand on the path and block my way.

"Get," I say.

Ssssss, they say.

They press forward, and I see every one has the face of the fourth-floor admin girl. Their flat black eyes are full of hate.

"Why didn't you call?" they honk mournfully. "Why didn't you call?"

They nip at my legs, quick as snakes. I stumble, and the path flicks me forward. The world wants to swallow me; the weedy woods gape like a mouth.

With all my pathetic strength I yank my feet free. I run back to the glass-walled cafeteria and slip in through the closing door. Back through the carpeted halls, back to my barren cube.

There are worse things than the gray safety of DR3.

I realize the way out is not the door.

It hits me: I need to cross over, or whatever. I rack my brain for everything I know about dy— about what I am.

Ghost. Patrick Swayze had to save his girlfriend. I don't have a girlfriend, not anymore. It's too late to get one, unless I find some transparent PR chick floating around DR1.

Poltergeist. I haven't seen it since I was eight. Pieces emerge from memory: the midget psychic lady. The hot daughter who died in real life. The TV. The portal was the TV.

Might as well try it. I drift downstairs to the lobby. The back wall is covered with plasma flat-screens that play company commercials over and over, an endless loop of grinning red-shirts pitching DSLRs and Blu-ray players. I flatten myself against them like a moth. I feel the radiation, a heat that does not warm. And nothing.

The Sixth Sense. What was Bruce Willis' deal? He had to help the kid. That's the reason he got stuck. Because he felt guilty, he had something left to do.

What do I have left to do?

The only thing I can think of. The thing I've been meaning to do for months.

I race back to my cube. There's the resignation letter, folded in thirds, under the stack of blender specs and merchant requests. I see the corner sticking out. I wrote it, didn't I? Why didn't that count?

No one read it. My manager needs to read it.

I haunt my cube for days, waiting for someone to find the letter. Maybe when they come to steal my stapler? It's a Bostitch, got a nice heft to it. The office supply cabinet is empty.

No one takes the stapler. No one clears my desk. There are rumors in the air about more layoffs. The promised turnaround, the one they gathered us in rented tents to explain, isn't coming. I am all but forgotten.

Then, she comes. The fourth-floor admin, the one with a muffin top and lank shaggy hair. The one with long incisors she hides by never smiling. The Mastodon, the guys called her. I laughed when they said it. I denied I ever kissed her.

I love the sight of her now.

She's trundling a cart, humming under her breath. She grunts a little as she lifts my desktop onto the cart, then the monitor. She turns the keyboard upside down, raps it and makes a *hmph* sound as greasy crumbs fall to the floor.

She begins sweeping everything else—my pen holder, my post-its, my folders— not onto the cart but into the trash. The trash. She works methodically, left to right, still humming what sounds like Donna Summers.

"Mm-*mm*-mm-*mm* stayin' alive," she hums, switching her hips back and forth. My letter's right there. The trash can's almost full.

Wait, I plead. *Wait a second. Please.*

She puts the stapler neatly on the cart. I am standing behind her, close as a lover. I lay my wisp of a hand on hers.

Please, I say.

She picks up the letter. Unfolds it. Scans it. Her lips twist in a strange smile.

And she drops it into the trashcan, along with everything else.

Bitch. Oh, you dirty bitch.

She trundles away with the cart, still humming that godawful tune.

I collapse on the crumb-gritted carpet like a jellyfish on the sand. A terrible, terrible word hangs above me.

Forever.

I will be at Circuit City forever.

Months pass.

I go down to tech support and watch softcore porn over programmers' shoulders. I read the spreadsheets scattered on accountants' desks and learn that things are much worse than anyone suspects. But mostly, I haunt the people I hate.

Boatshoes is at the top of my list. That asshole didn't even try CPR.

For days I sit on his spare swivel chair and stare. Just stare unblinking at the back of his head. He whips his head around, his eyes wide. Sometimes I lean closer and exhale a cold mist until I see the hairs rise on the back of his neck. I nudge his paranoia to the most exquisite pitch. But all that happens is he pops a few Xanax and spends the day working on his fantasy football draft.

Waxlip I haunt because he should have fired me months ago, back when that temp filed a complaint about the harassment. I wasn't harassing her, not really. She thought I was funny. She said so. But anyway, Waxlip should have fired me then. Then I'd be sitting on the porch with a beer right now instead of stuck in this fucking glue trap of a company.

For Waxlip I have a special trick. I lay my hand over his and I twitch the mouse the wrong way. Just a millimeter, is all I can manage, but it's enough. He clicks the wrong file, again and again, until he picks up the phone in fury and orders some poor IT guy to fix his fucking piece of shit PC.

I leave the fourth-floor admin alone. I'm not mad about the letter. Karma, I guess. Maybe that means the Buddhists have it right. Maybe I'll get reincarnated. I hope I get to be an otter, not an earwig.

I haunt the marketing specialist who said my idea for the Game Cave Sweepstakes was lame. I haunt the cafeteria lady who bitched at me when I said the lettuce in my sandwich was rotten. I haunt the Director of Social Media Initiatives, just for the hell of it.

I whisper hideous things into the HVAC system.

What else do I have to do?

November brings my last hope. The hallways hum; the big one is coming. I watch people clear screenplays from their desktops. I watch them sneak home the Denon speakers and 200-gig hard drives they were never supposed to have in the first place.

I watch an HR lady with cropped blonde hair make the rounds of the fourth floor. "Your manager needs to see you," she tells each one in turn. The meetings are brief. Hugs are forbidden. The HR lady gives each person one corrugated box. The cardboard flaps whisper as they close.

The survivors, huddled in their cubes, shoot the HR lady looks of loathing. They don't know that later, she hides in the conference room and sobs. I see it. I see it all. I follow her back to her gray office and watch over her shoulder as she grimly updates the payrolls. The names blur by. Am I there? Am I a glitch, a blip, to be cleared up?

The HR lady stays until 7. She calls her husband and says she'll be home by 9. There's a mudslide at Bennigan's with her name on it.

I am still here.

A few days after the layoffs, the company announces its Chapter 11 reorg. The CC symbol falls off the stock exchange. My thin heart leaps.

The CEO vows to keep the stores open. Business limps on. The Black Friday frenzy comes and goes. Christmas, too. Sales aren't bad, I hear. But they're not good enough.

No savior leaps to buy the vast unwieldy company. The VPs sigh and unfurl their parachutes.

There's no one in the halls now. The cafeteria is closed. The lobby TVs have been ripped out; wires dangle from the wall. The stores are still open. Clearance, Final Days. When is my final day? When the last "Fantastic Four" DVD leaves the shelf?

In March, I watch the last one leave. It's the old lady who sat at the security desk. I watch her totter out to the parking lot, heels clicking on the asphalt. Click click click.

The halls of Circuit City are silent.

There's no one left to haunt. My hate wilts.

I spend weeks drifting in the glass-walled corridor that connects DR1 to DR3, watching two robins build a nest on the gutterspout. One morning three deer walk out into the courtyard, delicately sniffing the air. The geese have flown.

With longing eyes I trace the asphalt trail across the overgrown lawn. I follow it until it plunges into shadow and vanishes into the woods. I think about how many times I'd planned to go running there. Running. I could never bring myself to do it. Could never make myself change clothes in the stinking men's room and then trot along the trail, dodging the women in stockings and white sneakers.

I wish I could run. More than anything else, I want to run. But the door is locked, and the woods fill me with a nameless dread.

So I drift back and forth, waiting for something to happen. A maintenance man shows up sometimes. He's the only one who kept his job. Real estate agents trip lightly down the hall, trilling about 400,000 square feet and stain-resistant gray carpet.

I don't know what I'm waiting for. Not anymore. Maybe for a signature on some obscure document, dissolving the last shreds of the company. Or for a long-toothed admin to forgive.

I know, deep down, that neither is true. I will be here in DR3 until the concrete crumbles. Until the very memory of this place is gone.

Until the day of final liquidation.

We're History

Rebecca Snow

The houselights came up, and I stood, stretching my arms above my head. The ripped, red seat creaked with relief as a spring popped. The duct taped repair job left marks on the backs of my legs, but the Byrd Theatre's majestic opulence and screening of The Evil Dead made the inconveniences worthwhile. Cracking my neck, I waited as a crowd of college kids exited the row.

"She's your girlfriend," a tall, freckled boy laughed. "You deal with her."

"Ha. Ha," a pink-haired girl said as she leaned up and smacked him on the back of the head.

Their banter faded as I tilted my head from side to side watching the colored lights twinkle in the chandelier. If the fixture ever fell during a movie, it would crush a lot of people. I always sat on the right when I came to watch a feature, out of the path of destruction.

My little brother Joey was gaming at One Eyed Jacques until midnight, so I wasn't in any hurry. Contemplating my watch, I saw he wouldn't be ready for over an hour. Our parents had died six-months before, and I had become my eleven-year-old brother's guardian. Even though the game ran later than I thought he should be awake, I made allowances for things he enjoyed.

A few restaurants were still open for business, but my stomach was full of popcorn. I pushed the polished brass bar on the door and stepped into the night. Even if the shops were closed, I figured I might as well do some window shopping while I waited.

A woman sat beneath the marquee playing a guitar. She smiled as she sang a quiet tune I didn't know. I threw a couple dollars in her open guitar case and walked a few steps to gaze into a window filled with vintage dresses. One gown glittered with sequins and made me think of a costume party I was supposed to attend. I had planned to wear an orange shirt that proclaimed, "This IS my costume." After seeing the shimmering frock, I reconsidered.

The New York Deli came into view, and I realized the popcorn hadn't been as filling as I'd thought. Pushing open the door, I saw the coeds from the theater.

"Kandar! Kandar!" they chanted at a table by the window before laughing and returning to their menus.

Other than the small group of movie lovers, the place was less crowded than I'd expected. Most Fridays found the restaurant congested at best. I took a seat at the bar. A lanky young barkeep slid to a stop and caught my eye.

"What can I do for you?" he asked, wiping an invisible spill with a dishcloth.

"Can I get some fries and a lemonade?"

"That all?" He raised his eyebrows.

I nodded and turned to survey the room. A couple fell out of the photo booth and howled with laughter. Clinging to each other and snickering, they waited for their film to emerge. I would have bet anything that they'd never show the thin sheet of pictures to their grandkids. A figure sprinted past the front window in the direction of the Byrd.

"I wonder whose purse he stole," I mumbled.

"Excuse me?" the barman said, placing my order in front of me.

"Oh, nothing. Just commenting on city rabble." I squinted down the counter and didn't see what I needed. "Can I have some ketchup?"

He went back to the kitchen and returned with a small plastic cup. Wiping his hands on a folded apron, he stood watching the front of the restaurant. I dipped a fry in the red goo and popped it into my mouth before turning to follow his gaze. Three more people ran past.

"What do you think?" he asked tilting his chin toward the turmoil outside.

I shrugged and ate another sliced potato.

"None of my business." If there was one thing I couldn't stand, it was rubber-neckers on the highway tying up traffic for miles. The same went for gawkers at a crime scene.

I took a sip of my lemonade. Before I could set the tumbler back on the counter, one of the runners slammed into the front glass leaving a glistening red smear where he'd collided. The man's wide eyes looked at the giant smudge as if it were poison before he tripped back into a limping jog.

Downing the last of my drink, I puckered my lips to hide the sour grimace, dropped a ten-dollar bill on the bar, and grabbed a fry for the road. If the accident had happened up the street, I thought Joey might be in trouble.

The second I opened the door, the music from the bar drowned in sirens and horns. A small fire that must have been blazing near Martin's shot sparks into the air. Screams pierced the night behind me. I had to get to Joey.

I ran against the current of people escaping from the direction of the flames. Some were bloody. Others leaned on or half-carried friends. All of them looked as though they'd seen Bigfoot abducted by a UFO. Pressing myself against one of Mongrel's windows to let a group of wounded pass, I saw a cat dish I'd have to come back to buy. Once the way was clear, I dashed to the corner and crossed the street before the next wave of wounded clogged my path. A pale man coughed up what looked like a lung full of blood and fell to his knees. A woman I suspected was his wife dropped next to him.

"Get away," someone yelled from the crowd. "He's changing."

Arms reached out of the group to rescue the lady from her companion.

"No, just leave me!" she shrieked. "Jim's gonna be fine once he gets his breath." She turned to him and placed a hand on his back. "Won't you, Pookie?" Her voice raised an octave on the pet name. "We'll catch up."

Jim waved her away and then collapsed into the blood he'd just expelled. The woman tried to drag him back to his feet. Only managing to grunt him into a sitting position, she looked up at the dispersing crowd.

"Isn't somebody gonna help?" she squealed. "I can't lift him by myself."

The man's torso jerked. The group crumbled into a fragment of runners. Before I could make a move, Jim flailed his arms and grasped the woman in a bear hug. Burying his face in her neck, he bit a chunk from her throat and chewed. She didn't have time to scream.

I took two tentative steps backward before I had the courage to edge past the scene and duck into the darkened entrance alcove of Plan 9 Music. The store wasn't open, but the dim surroundings hid me. If I had seen the incident on the news, I would have never believed it. Having been flecked by the woman's blood and having glimpsed the genuine fear in the fleeing revelers, my usual skepticism faded.

I took a few deep breaths before I peeked from the shadows. Jim and the woman he'd mauled stumbled to their feet in pursuit of the mob that had abandoned them. They hobbled half a block before I crept from my hiding place. I was a little over half a block from the game store and my brother. For the moment, the sidewalk was free of obstacles. I could have run, but I slunk across the closed storefronts to avoid attracting attention.

When I came to North Belmont, I had to leave the relative safety of overhangs and doorways and step into the glow of the streetlamps. Ignoring the red crosswalk signal, I stooped low and ran past a three-car pileup. A teenager pressed his bloody face on an unbroken windshield as I passed. He pawed the glass with a handful of crooked fingers.

I passed one last darkened store before I made it to the

entrance of One Eyed Jacques and peered through the glass. About fourteen gamers loitered in the back of the store. I pressed my back against the door.

Surveying the street, I saw a mass of people gathered around the windows of the Galaxy Diner. From my vantage point, I couldn't tell if they were perpetrators or victims. After quick deliberation, I wasn't sure there was a difference. The gathering seemed intent on gaining entrance.

I eased open the door to the game store and squeezed through the smallest gap I could manage. The woman behind the counter raised an eyebrow in my direction.

"Can I help you?" she asked.

"I'm here for my brother, Joey."

The woman's face erupted in a smile bright enough to make the sun jealous.

"He's such a good kid. He plays well with the others, even if he is a lot younger."

I nodded, leaned against the wall, and gasped to catch my breath.

"You need to block this door," I said, panting.

The woman's grin faded as she re-arched her brow. I tugged at a heavy display, but it wouldn't budge with my feeble attempt.

"Mike," she called. "Some nut job's trying to make me close the store."

I felt a hand grip my shoulder and spin me sideways.

"Can I help you?" the hand's owner growled.

"You can help me block the door," I said pressing my palms to my forehead. "I don't know what's going on out there, but there's a fire up the street, and I just saw a man rip out a woman's voice box with his teeth."

"Calm down," the man said. To the woman, he added, "Call the police."

I continued to yank on the case without it so much as a wiggling.

"Mike, it's busy," the woman said. "Nine-one-one is busy."

A gore-covered woman picked that moment to slam her face into the window. Mike jumped back, thrusting his hand into a stack of games to block his fall. They all tumbled to the floor.

"Margaret, lock the door." Mike scrambled to his feet and threw his back against the game wall. An avalanche of boxes tumbled from the shelves. "Now."

Margaret left her perch behind the counter and hurried to the door with a jingling ring of keys. Gripping the pull bar, she twisted the lock as the horrific woman outside dragged a hand down the glass leaving a dripping stain in its wake. The ripped hem of a sleeve snagged the handle. Had Margaret not locked the door when she did, the monster would have shuffled inside the store. The door jumped as the fiend tried to free its arm. Recovering his faculties, Mike leaned over and unlocked the wheels on the display I had been wrestling and rolled it in front of the exit. He reached to the wall and flicked a switch that dimmed the front of the store.

"Hey, it's only eleven," a familiar voice said.

I saw Joey's head turn and pop up from among the other

gamers. His eyes lit when he saw me before his brow creased into a frown.

"What's wrong?" he asked.

"I grab Thorabald's treasure and dump it in my bag of holding," a boy a bit older than Joey said.

"I think you'd better put the game on hold," I said as I ruffled his hair.

"Can't do it, I'm not the dungeon master," Joey said and pointed to a guy about nineteen wearing a red bandana with an eyeball sewn onto it. "Bill is."

"Bill, I think it's time to call it quits for the night," I said.

Bill raised his eyes from a dice roll before his head followed his gaze. He gave me a pinched grin that made him look as if he'd smelled his own sock drawer.

"I...don't...think...so," he said. "We have the place until closing. And that's not for another hour. Right guys?"

He looked around the table. Several players nodded in solidarity.

Margaret swept past me and whispered into Bill's ear. She must have said magic words because he slammed shut the books in front of him and began gathering papers into a yellow folder.

"Okay, guys," he said not looking up. "We're done for the night. I'll tally the points and shoot you all an e-mail by Wednesday."

"Aw, man," a blond girl said. "I was supposed to get my dragon."

"My mom won't be here for another hour," a bespectacled redhead said.

Mike stepped up to the table as the gamers packed their gear.

"We have a situation," he said as he placed both hands flat on the table. "This is not a drill, and I expect you to follow orders."

The paper shuffling ceased as the troupe stared at the large man.

"From the looks of it, we have zombies," Mike said.

I had to admit I was surprised when, instead of gasping in horror, the small crowd squealed in delight. What was more disturbing to me was that I hadn't thought of it first.

"I don't know how long we'll be here, but I need you all to call your parents or loved ones. We need to know the situation." Mike wiped his face with a red bandana.

"Hey, Mike," I said, tapping the man on the shoulder. "Does this place have a back door?"

He nodded and pointed to the storeroom.

"I don't think it's safe out there," he said. "You'd have a better chance of survival staying here."

I glanced at the crowd of swaying dead collecting at the front window in spite of Mike's efforts to darken the store.

"My car's on Ellwood, and home isn't too far away."

Mike shrugged and held out an ornamental Samurai sword.

"Here. Take this." He thrust the faux weapon into my hands.

I wasn't sure it would cut paper, but the man meant well. I

nodded and gripped the hilt and scabbard to unsheathe the blade. It glimmered in the fluorescent lighting.

"Just make sure to close that door behind you," he said, tossing Joey a baseball bat.

My brother caught the bat one-handed and slung his gaming bag over his shoulder.

"Keep in touch, guys," Joey said as he followed me through the dimness of the back room.

Pressing my ear to the door, I listened but heard nothing. I eased open the door and peered into the lot. Anything could have been hiding around the parked cars. I strained my ears. No footsteps shuffled in the gravel, so I stepped into the open air.

"C'mon." I motioned for Joey to follow. "The car's this way."

Instead of crossing the street, we edged between two duplexes. A dog barked at us from a back yard. Sirens wailed in the distance. Screams peppered the neighborhood. As we neared the end of the tight corridor, a figure staggered into view. It lifted its head as if it were sampling the air. I froze. Joey bumped into my back, throwing me off balance. I pounded my hand on the side of the building to steady myself. The thud echoed down the alleyway. The monster exhaled a hungry moan as its head snapped toward us. I pushed Joey behind me and held the sword toward the creature. Joey squeaked. Behind him, another zombie blocked the entrance to the passage.

"We could try walking up the side of the building with our backs pressed together," he said.

I tossed him a quick smile. I admired his quick thinking even though I knew his legs were too short to make the idea plausible. If there had been a window close, we could have broken it and climbed inside and explained the damage to the homeowners. As far as I could see, the walls were bare of anything but siding.

Joey jumped from behind me and lifted the wooden bat above his head. Heaving a primal scream that seemed to contain all of the anger and hurt from the loss of our parents, he slammed it down on the approaching shuffler's head. The body dropped, but Joey kept smashing the ash wood into the corpse's skull. I let him go and turned to face the danger blocking our escape. Drawing back the glorified letter opener, I did what I never thought I'd be able to do. I pressed the tip deep into the beast's eye socket and wiggled the blade. The head fell limp before the cadaver fell to the dirt. Joey had stopped shrieking, but he continued to blast the bloody mess to a mushier pulp.

Avoiding the bat, I wrapped my arms around my brother and squeezed him until his struggling lessened. He turned to me and sobbed into my collar.

"Shh," I said. "You saved my life." I smoothed his bangs back as I pushed his face away from my neck. "Time for us to get out of here."

His legs wobbled as I released my grip. We scanned the street. The only movement was over a block away. I pressed my key fob and heard the car doors unlock. The parking lights flashed two cars from where we stood. Opening the driver's door, I pushed Joey inside before I followed.

"Seatbelt," I said without thinking.

"I know. I've seen the movie." Joey snapped the restraint in place as I turned the ignition.

The car rocked as a giant ball of flame lit up the sky. Joey jerked.

"What was that?" he asked, his eyes glowing in the lights from the dash.

"I'd guess that'd be the Seven-Eleven next to Ellwood Thompson's," I said. "I'm glad I got gas before we came out tonight."

I took two rights and drove through the neighborhoods toward Boulevard. Our best bet was to get out of the city on back streets.

"So, Kiddo, you've been fighting zombies, where do you want to go?" I asked.

"Not home." Joey picked at a loose thread on his jeans.

I swerved to avoid a downed tree branch.

"Okay, where then?"

Joey scratched his head. "Let's go to the beach." He turned and flashed me a wide grin.

"Which one?"

I slowed the car to pass a group of feasting creatures. One raised its head and made a move to stand. I pressed the accelerator.

"I don't think it matters." Joey shrugged and watched the darkened streets.

As we wound our way out of town, I caught glimpses in the rearview mirror of fireballs rising from the city.

"I wonder what they'll write in the history books about the burning of Richmond this time."

Joey craned his neck to look behind us.

"I wonder who'll be left to write them." He flopped back in his seat and closed his eyes.

Dirt and Iron

Dawn Terrizzi

When the Church Hill Tunnel fell on a dreary October day in 1925, I was standing directly behind Locomotive 231, facing west on one of the flat cars trailing behind, having just relieved myself of a large trough of dirt. Jack Daley was working nearby on the roof of the tunnel. Both of us were on the team hired to widen the tunnel that housed a mile-long track, part of the railroad system running some 4000 miles from Richmond to what is now Huntington, West Virginia.

Completed in 1875, the Church Hill Tunnel lay beneath present-day Jefferson Park and had fallen into disuse in the early 1900s due to various problems with its construction. One main problem was that the tunnel was prone to seepage since the hill that it ran through was made up of blue marl clay instead of the more common and more secure bedrock. A distinctive characteristic of blue marl clay is that it does not absorb water well and becomes very slippery when wet.

On that rainy day in October, Locomotive 231 entered the eastern side of the tunnel, hauling behind it ten empty flat cars. Just as the train passed below 20th Street, some of the bricks holding up the tunnel shifted and fell, knocking out the power in the tunnel. Panicking, workers inside the tunnel began running around in the darkness. Some fled toward the daylight at the tunnel's ends, while some had only enough time to jump beneath a flatcar to save themselves before more rocks slipped. Many men were able to find their way out of the tunnel in the few minutes between the power outage and the tunnel's complete collapse.

My eyes never had time to adjust to the darkness, as I was immediately knocked from the train car by something heavy. The lamp on my helmet blew out and I lay on the ground, stunned. I was, however, able to get up after a few seconds. I stood there in the darkness and heard my fellow workers shouting and moaning. I heard more rocks fall and a horrible noise behind me. Something exploded. I was frozen for a moment, not sure where to go. My brain quickly kicked my body into motion and I scrambled blindly over rocks and debris. My nose began to run and strangely I felt like laughing. This was not supposed to happen.

Another couple of rocks fell somewhere to my left and I jumped. I climbed and sweated and cursed. I heard a noise that made me pause and I struggled to catch my breath. Jack came up beside me on my right. His headlamp was still working and as he gazed into my face I saw his eyes round with shock. We heard another crunch from above and knew we didn't have much time left. We leaned our bodies forward into escape. However, Jack was quicker than me and as he pushed off the ground, he dislodged a rock from a nearby pile. The rock rolled right into my path and I fell hard on my right arm. I cursed in pain.

As I cradled my arm and made a move to get up, a sudden shift in the tunnel's ceiling made a large cement block come rushing down. It landed directly on the backs of my legs. I yelled out in both pain and surprise and raised my head to find help.

"Jack!" I cried. I needed someone to move the block. I couldn't do it myself.

Jack stopped and turned around. His eyes were still wide and his breathing was heavy. He looked at my legs and then at the ceiling for what seemed like forever. His gaze traveled back down and rested briefly on my face. Then he turned and ran.

"Jaaack!" I howled. Between my arm and my trapped legs, I was pinned into place. I struggled with my good arm to twist my body and push the block from my legs. I grunted through pain and frustration. I couldn't reach it. I hit the ground and cried. I heard a groan from above. I tried again to free myself. After another few seconds, the whole section of tunnel above me collapsed completely.

I felt a rush of air on my face from the cascading dirt and something sharp scraped my cheek on its way down. I felt a heavy blow on my head and was thrust into insensibility.

I regained consciousness a short while later and slowly remembered what had happened and where I was. The only way I knew I wasn't dead was the horrendous throbbing in my head. I had a small pocket of air around my upper body and a small cavern of space to my left. I could not move anything except my one good arm, and I could only move that a little. My abdomen was tight and sore. I blinked dust from my eyes and wished I had some water.

I attempted without success to shift my aching body. I cried out as pain shot through my back. I slumped back into the same position and my thoughts drifted to my family and my wife. A lone tear escaped my left eye and I felt relief as the moisture briefly cradled my raw eye. Within moments, I fell into an uncomfortable slumber.

I was awakened by a spasm of coughing. It felt like my lungs were on fire and I felt pain as I never have before. I guessed that I had some broken ribs. When I stopped coughing, I felt what had to have been blood beneath my mouth. I swallowed and a clot of blood slithered down my throat and I almost vomited. I closed my eyes and breathed slowly. I wanted to cry. I had no idea how long I'd been down here or how long it would take me to die.

As the pain in my lungs subsided, I thought about being rescued. Was it possible? Would the city try to rescue me or would the attempt cause further damage? My family would miss me if I wasn't found. I would miss them. I would miss my home, my books, my bed. My comfortable bed with pillows and a blanket. From my bed I could look out the window and see the large oak tree with its squirrels and birds and leaves. Some nights I would sit next to the open window to relax. My eyes began to feel heavy. I thought of the pots in my kitchen and the side table next to my couch in the sitting room. My eyes drooped. Something sour escaped from between my lips. I slept and awoke with fever.

I heard something that I wasn't sure was real or in my mind. It was a scritchy sound, a sound like two coarse rags being rubbed slowly together. The sound made me feel itchy and tired. I couldn't move my neck, but my eyes slid back and forth in the darkness. My heart beat wildly and I felt like screaming. Where was the noise coming from? It seemed in front of me, yet all around me at the same time. It gradually became louder and I closed my eyes against the sound that was a train car in my head, a fall of rocks, the slide of dirt, the screams of men. Just as I thought my head would burst, the sound stopped. I breathed deeply, opened my eyes, and jerked back. Something brushed against my face. I felt a warm sensation on my left thigh. I still had feeling in my thigh. Something whispered in my ear. I couldn't make out the words. I breathed. I waited.

Another thing brushed against my body. This time against my hand. Something was on my hand. Was I being rescued?

I moaned. My back hurt, my head hurt, my belly hurt. I couldn't feel the bottom half of my legs. But I felt myself smile as something grabbed my other hand. It felt smooth and cold. The coldness felt good on my hand and spread over my body. Then I was shivering. But the thing held on. My mother used to hold my hands when I was sick as a child. She would sing and rub my hand as I slept. I could feel her presence in my sleep when I was a child. I could feel her right now. I smelled dirt and iron. I saw a light and a hand and a crowd of men peering down at me. They did not have any faces. Only blackness where their faces should be. I heard voices and then the scritchy sound again. I vomited. I urinated. I waited. I saw Locomotive 231. It was staring at me, laughing at me for how little ways I had actually made it when I tried to escape and how far I had felt I had gone. I thought I was leaving the engine far behind me when all this time it was right beside me, mocking me. The engine smelled of flesh and fire. I heard its whistle. Its whistle sang a death song. I screamed.

Jack made it out of the tunnel with only a few bruises. He fell to the ground and some of his fellow workers rushed over to check on him. They hauled him up and pat him on the back while he coughed and spat.

The world blurred and everything got quiet. Jack thought of what had happened, what he had done. He too should have died that day.

The men hustled him into a waiting ambulance and hurried back to the scene. Another ambulance had already taken fireman Ben Mosby to Grace Hospital. Ben, horribly burned when the train engine's boiler exploded, would die bloody and in shock later that night from his irreparable injuries.

In the days following the tragedy, the city tried numerous rescue attempts for the men who had been trapped inside the tunnel. Recovered engineer Tom Mason, killed instantly, was found pinned to the throttle of his train when his rescuers arrived. The men that were in the collapse and survived often spoke of that day in whispers, as if heard talking about it would curse them. One year after the collapse, in 1926, the tunnel would be deemed unsafe, filled with sand and sealed up at both ends. Inside the sealed hillside, there rested Locomotive 231 and the bodies of the men who were not recovered.

Jack returned to his regular life soon after the incident. His wife had insisted that he spend a few days recovering at home before returning to work. He did not help with the recovery effort. He was transferred to another project in the next county and chose not to go back to the disaster site for the memorial ceremony the city held in honor of those who had died.

It was exactly three months after the fall of the Church Hill Tunnel that Jack began experiencing the dizziness and the headaches. He would get up in the morning and feel fine. But then slowly, throughout the morning, dizziness would overtake Jack's body and the headaches would creep in unnoticed until

Jack couldn't remember a time that he didn't feel this way. After a while, Jack's job performance was so awful that his boss had no choice but to let him go.

The night he was fired, Jack's wife suggested that he see a doctor.

"Honey, it's nothing to worry about."

"Dammit, Jack. You wouldn't have been fired had it not been for those episodes."

Jack looked down at his hands. "Yes," he said quietly, "I know."

So Jack went to a doctor. The doctor was thorough and ran many tests but could find nothing physically wrong.

"You know son," the doctor said, "from what you told me, it's unlikely that there is anything physically wrong with your head. It's probably just stress. I'm sure you've been under a lot of it." After he said this, the doctor paused and peered at Jack from over the rims of his glasses.

Jack didn't say anything. He felt sick and his head ached.

The doctor's voice was gentle. "Go take it easy for a few days and you'll feel better in no time."

Jack dragged himself back home and climbed into bed. He was glad that he had some money saved from an inheritance for him and his wife to live on while he was out of work. He sighed from exhaustion and closed his eyes. Jack was on the edge of sleep when something abruptly woke him. He flew up into a sitting position, feeling scared and disoriented. He didn't know what had woken him, but he felt strange. As if someone had pushed him off his bed in mid-sleep. He had a sensation of falling. His head spun.

Just then he heard someone call his name. He looked around, his eyes wide with fear. The voice called his name again and this time Jack believed it was coming from his small backyard. Jack swung his legs over the side of the bed and went to stand, but suddenly felt more disoriented than before. And then the seizure overtook him.

When Jack regained consciousness, he found himself lying on the floor. He pulled himself up, confused and sore.

"Jack!" The voice. It was back. Jack began to shake.

"Jack? You in here?" His wife. It was only his wife.

"Nina!"

"Oh my God, Jack! What happened to you!" His wife rushed to his side and grabbed his arm. He wobbled as her weight pushed against him. "Honey," she said fearfully, "what on earth is happening to you?"

He shook his head. "I don't know."

Nina looked up at him with tears in her eyes. "You should lie down." She sniffed.

He lay in bed all afternoon, but got no sleep.

The next time it happened, Jack and Nina were taking a short walk outside. Jack had been inside for much of the week and a walk seemed a welcome change. The day was clear and fresh. Jack was pointing at a small white rabbit that had positioned himself under a tree in the field they were passing.

"Nina, look. I've hardly – ever - seen a wh- wha- ba-rrr..." Jack's language became garbled and his eyes became wide.

"Jack? Jack, what's happening?" Nina cried.

He fell to the ground as convulsions tore through his body. His hands became tight and his fingers twisted into impossible positions. His mouth leaked horrible sounds and his breathing was heavy and strained.

Nina flopped onto the ground next to Jack and looked around for help. The road was empty. "Help!" she called, crying. "Please, help!"

No one came.

Gradually his body began to relax and his breathing evened. Nina was sitting next to him, crying, and holding his hand. "Jack?"

Jack's eyes took a minute to focus on his wife. "Nina? What happened?" His speech was slurred.

"I think you had a seizure. We need to get you to the hospital."

Over the next few days Jack was again subjected to tests. The doctors found nothing wrong. They told him that what he experienced must not have truly been a seizure. They told him to come back the following week for further testing, assuring Jack and his wife that he was in no immediate danger.

That night, Jack had another seizure. When he arose the next morning, he felt extremely tired and his head was foggy. He decided to lie back down. He fell immediately to sleep.

The corridor was long and Jack was tired of walking. Every time he turned a corner, he thought he would see the end of the passage, yet every turn only yielded more passage. He dragged his feet and listened to the sound of them scraping the floor. The passage was quiet except for one faraway noise that Jack could not make out. The corridor was hot and stuffy and Jack found it hard to breathe. Turn after turn after turn. Finally, he turned a corner and stopped abruptly in front of a window. Yawning, as an attempt to catch his breath, Jack stared out the window into endless night.

A loud noise woke Jack from his dream. He sat up in bed and looked toward the window. A dark shape moved on the other side. Jack briefly noticed that he felt pretty good. His exhaustion was gone and his head felt clearer than it had in days.

He threw back the blanket and climbed out of bed, his eyes following the shadow outside. He walked slowly to the window. His breathing quickened and he felt afraid.

He reached the window and pulled back the curtain. He didn't see anything. Something about his reflection, though, caught his eye. It slowly became distorted. He saw his belly, his chest, his arms, his face. His face. When he looked back up, it was not his face that he saw in the glass. But he knew this face. The last time he had seen it was in the tunnel, right before he had made the decision to flee. The face looked at him, its eyes showing amusement. The lips formed a smile and then the mouth opened.

"Jaaack..." The voice was light and airy, yet held something dark and mocking underneath.

"Jaaack..." Dirt spilled out of the open mouth.

"No." Jack stepped back and reached to pull the curtain shut.

A strong force knocked him onto his back. He stared up into the face of the man he had left to die.

"Jaaack..."

Jack's scream was cut short as piles and piles of dirt slid over his body and poured into his mouth. He choked and coughed and flailed his arms. He wiggled onto his side and saw where he was. He was no longer in his bedroom at home. He was back in the tunnel.

Maggie

Amber Timmerman

The worst ideas begin as insignificant, germinating thoughts. They end with rather hideous habits.

Michael Pearce knew, and could not seem to willfully forget, that a person's body contains more microbial cells than human ones. Freshly showered or not, people are mostly, by percentage, bacteria. And the same parasites that are happy to munch on the food coming down a gullet, are just as happy to munch on the gullet itself once the host has expired.

The consequence of this information was that Michael preferred to touch things while wearing a pair of surgical gloves, which were as thin as rice paper and softer than actual skin. He thought of them as hand condoms, really, and though he was self-conscious about the way they looked, he almost never took them off.

The dimmed lights of the restaurant twinkled above them in a forcibly unflattering manner, and he tried very hard not to notice the dark stain on the top right hand corner of the tablecloth.

"Pass the bread?"

"Of course."

Also, it had come to his attention that the great majority of people were not in the habit of looking at themselves up close, and in the course of investigating this phenomenon, he had developed a bit of a staring problem. His observations revealed that people tended to groom themselves as though they were mainly going to be viewed from far away, leaving countless overlooked flaws, some more glaring than others.

His date smiled a lot, and when she did, tiny folds marked their territory on the places where they would one day take up permanent residence, so that he could see exactly what she would look like in twenty years. She hadn't been hydrating properly. He also didn't care for the topography of creases on her neck; it was like she had managed to make it into her thirties without once buckling under the intense peer pressure and sagely wisdom of Cosmopolitan magazine.

Still, dating was about compromise.

"What's with the gloves?" she asked.

It was an inevitable question, and he was used to it. He had spent the past three years disregarding the sideways glances of friends and strangers, who never seemed to sort out whether they should be alarmed or merely concerned. So, on the sensible grounds that a sudden education in Lister's germ theory tended to put people off their lunch, he gave his traditional, rehearsed response: "I think they lend a sense of occasion to things, don't you?"

But she didn't exactly laugh.

"I guess," she said, popping a sizeable bit of cheddar biscuit through the opening of her chapped lips. "They're kind of weird."

"You know, the story of surgical gloves is really kind of a love story," he added, reflectively. "They were commissioned by the chief surgeon William Halsted in 1890 to protect the sensitive hands of his lover, Caroline Hampton, because she was allergic to the carbolic acid they used to sterilize instruments. It became a worldwide staple in modern medicine and ended up saving countless lives."

She harrumphed. "Well, you can't get diamonds every time."

"They did eventually get married."

The word *married* dangled between them like a worm twisting violently at the end of an indifferent hook.

"So, I'm going to VCU right now for a communications major," she said, by way of dispelling the worm, "but I think I might change my mind and go into social work. There are just a lot of, like, needy people out there, you know? But basically I'd have to start all over in school, so... Are you going anywhere?"

"Going anywhere?"

"Yeah, like, university-wise."

Michael wondered if the person making the biscuits had worn plastic gloves. Not all restaurants used them. "Oh, I've already graduated," he said.

She chewed slowly on her mouthful, feigning thoughtful silence, pretending that she was still thinking of the next question she would ask. But it was obvious. She was going to ask him what he did for a living. Here it comes, he thought.

"So, what do you do now?"

Her predictability was disappointing.

Also, she had a great deal of cat hair on her blouse, much of which had become distressingly airborne, making the biscuits, definitively, too big of a risk. "I'm a mortician. Just started six months ago."

"Wow," she said, her mouth hanging open, revealing half-masticated dinner roll in the exposed crevices. "So you, like... cut open dead people?"

She was thinking of a medical examiner. Someone with the barest exposure to cable television should have known the difference. "I don't do autopsies or anything. It's nothing to do with figuring out how someone died. I prepare them for their funerals."

"So, you, like, dress them or something?"

In social situations, when he felt awkward, he relied on the diversionary tactics of fun facts. He wondered if she would be impressed to know that woodpeckers had tongues that wrapped completely around their brains.

Then the woman one booth over coughed violently into her fist, and like a vulture catching the early onset whiff of decay, he instinctively focused in on her.

That woman, pressing a tissue into her swollen, crinkled nose, her cotton-candy hair betraying a geriatric thinness under which mocha islands of melanoma shone through; she was not a woman who had ever bothered with sunscreen. Now only the business of her dermatologist and perhaps her Avon representative, it would soon be his, and he would be challenged to rectify a lifetime worth of bad UVA/UVB decisions. Or, take her husband, too busy disguising his spare tire stomach with the busyness of grey and black argyle to have remembered to trim the long hairs gathered into tiny brooms in his nostrils; only 3 snips away from looking presentable, and yet he couldn't be bothered. These details, infuriating in their ubiquitous repetition, person after person, consumed him.

"I also really like movies," he said, staring at the nostrils. "Particularly anything by Michel Gondry or Wes Anderson. I've got a huge collection."

Her eyes widened, and she nodded slightly in a way that assured him that she had not really been listening, and was instead focused on plumbing out a piece of biscuit that had become gummy in her molars. "So, you must really see, like, a lot of sad people, right? I mean, that sucks." She took a reflective moment to clean the impacted biscuit from under her nail and wipe it into her napkin. "I mean, it sucks that anyone should have to have that job. In the old days, those things just took care of themselves. People just dug a hole and that was that, huh?"

He wasn't sure to which old days she was referring, but he knew that a person left to decay on his own would soon be eaten from the inside out, the happy bacteria multiplying and defecating, until the body was bloated enough to rip at the seams. Gradually, the organs would liquefy, and brain matter would ooze out of the sunken mouth and ears, until there was nothing more substantial left than a sticky puddle.

Nature had absolutely no dignity; Michael Pearce was certain of this. No man should become a puddle of himself, and no bacteria should have the pleasure of getting in the last meal.

The waitress appeared with their entrees, coming so close when she set them down that he could smell her unwashed scalp.

He wondered how many of her skin cells had sloughed off in his salad. When she smiled at them, the tectonic plates of her face converged at their boundaries to make spectacular ridges, and showcased the volcanic mole on her bulbous cheek. He noticed, with what he hoped was discreet revulsion, that the errant mole had sprouted a hair. How could she have possibly missed a hair that long?

It had a curl in it.

Eating was now completely out of the question. He felt his pores open, nearly individually, and begin to excrete fluid. He felt the heat gathered in waves at his neck, the moisture soiling him. He cupped his hands around his water glass, feeling the coolness of it through his gloves like a salve.

"My theory is that pheromones are completely responsible for the chemistry between two people," he said, focusing on his uneven breath. "We're actually wired to mate with people who smell good to us. That good smell signals good genetic compatibility. Isn't that interesting?"

"You're a weird guy," she said, the blood of her steak soaking into her potatoes and broccoli. "I bet you're full of interesting facts and stories. I mean, with your job... Surrounded by horror, you must really have a dark side."

He wasn't sure whether to be flattered or suspicious. A dark side might bestow upon him a certain mysterious quality, but the word "horror" bothered him. It didn't seem like the sort of word that inspired after-dinner sex.

Sex.

One of the messiest of human activities, and one in which he had not participated in three years. Not since he had started learning the business.

He pressed a tomato with his fork until the skin popped and juice leaked out. He retracted the utensil and licked it. A shiver of its acid coated his mouth.

"I'm serious about the pheromones, though," he said. "All of our motivations, especially the biological ones, are directly controlled by our sense of smell."

"Like how you can get hungry just smelling an onion?"

"I guess," he mumbled. "Not really."

"You must be some sort of science geek," she said, giggling. "I guess you'd have to be, doing what you do."

"So, what kind of movies do you like?"

"I bet you can tell me just how it happens," she said, leaning forward so that her breasts pushed against the fabric of her neckline, "step by step. I bet it's totally twisted and dark too."

It was like that when he told people. Either they didn't want to talk about it or they wanted to know everything.

"Well," he said, stirring the dressing into his vegetables until they became a soup of themselves, "let's just say that the last bath you will ever have will be in a big metal tub, and you won't be the one holding the sponge."

"Wow," she said, a mouthful of warm meat, "that is like, totally morbid. You ever have to touch people that are, like; really fucked up?"

He didn't want to talk about his clients, or about how they

came to him in various states of disrepair, certain things crushed or disfigured, dehydrated and deflated, and in general, fatally defeated. Sometimes it was the fault of trauma or sickness, sometimes they were merely old, and sometimes they were just inexplicably ruined, like a cake that falls while baking.

The way she looked at him gave an actual sting to his sweat; he could feel an itch in his groin where his pants hugged him, and the olives in his salad looked like drowned roaches. He stopped staring at her to stare at his olives, half expecting them to make a swim for it.

It was the restaurant, he thought. It was too warm in there. She reached for her water and he saw that her cuticles were cracked and dry, and that there were chips in her mauve nail polish.

He began to feel the slightest panic, a maddeningly irresistible urge to go over her with a fine set of tweezers and a bag of solvents; an urge that needed to be crushed if he was going to make it through dinner and maybe on into a normal, healthy relationship.

"So, did you grow up around here?"

"Oh, yeah," she said. "I've lived in Richmond my whole life. Actually went to Saint Gertrude, if you can believe it. I think my dad wanted to keep me away from the real world as long as possible. Not that being in an all girls school kept us from seeing boys, or sneaking off to the bathroom to smoke cigarettes... Snuck over to Benedictine's, just two blocks away, you know, and lost my virginity when I was sixteen. Did you grow up here?"

"I was born in Nashville, Tennessee, but I've lived here for most of my life."

"Nashville, huh? Country music is okay, I guess. I've always wanted an excuse to wear a cowboy hat."

He watched her take the food down, visualized it as it would move down her esophagus and become soft in her gut sac.

He hated country music, and in his experience, only singers and tourists actually wore cowboy hats; it was one of the ways they were easily distinguishable in a 2nd Avenue herd.

"So, what made you want to be a mortician?"

He considered telling her about the specific challenges of oral mucosa, anaerobic microbiota, and maggots, but he suspected that she might not share his level of passion on the subject. "What made you want to be a social worker? Aside from the profusion of needy people, obviously."

She leaned back and narrowed her eyes at him, almost conspiratorially. "So, you don't want to tell me about your work, and that's cool, I guess. But in return, you've got to tell me something personal about yourself. Something you don't normally tell people. Something weird."

She stared at him, brimming with some private excitement, and he knew that this was supposed to be their big moment, the one where they each told some endearing, intimate anecdote designed to bond them in time for dessert. But what in the hell would he tell her? And why did it have to be something weird?

"Okay, scaredy cat," she said, pulling one shoulder back and sticking her nose in the air. "I'll go first. I've got the perfect story for you." She settled herself back in her seat, a lip of fat curling like a frown from her pinched waistline. "When I was ten years old my parents got me this purple Huffy, the one with a basket in front and bells on the handles like I asked for. I was allowed to ride as long as I wanted, just as long as I didn't leave the subdivision. But every day, I went a little farther and farther out. Pretty soon, I was gone whole afternoons, riding all over town. I always lied about where I had been, and I got away with it for three whole years until I got caught by my mom outside of Cabo's Bistro. I had never been more grounded in my life. But, anyway, the places I went were all special places to me because they were secret places, and my favorite, my absolute favorite, was Hollywood Cemetery."

Of course it was. A city that contained the marvelous Byrd Theater and the church where Patrick Henry gave his brilliant "give me liberty or give me death," speech, and she was a cemetery fan.

She broke to stare at him expectantly, clearly looking for a reaction, as though her fondness for the place was something that he was sure to appreciate.

The truth was, Michael was sometimes bothered by graveyards, and by Hollywood Cemetery particularly, whose baroque showmanship romanced every Virginian into believing that they were genuinely *cemetery people*. Some suitably sculpted angels and a pointy spire or two, and suddenly the ugliness of death was eclipsed by something decorative and romantic. It didn't reflect what death was like at all; it was a place to take pictures and have a chicken salad sandwich.

"But that's not the best part," she said, and she lowered her voice as though she were channeling the literary suspense of her fourth grade diary: "One time, on a dare, I lay down on top of this woman's grave." And here, she stifled a giggle. He could smell the butter of mashed potatoes on her breath. "I don't even remember her name, which is probably bad somehow, but I lay down anyways and closed my eyes. I just lay there, pretending that I was her. I stayed there for, like, ten whole minutes, imagining I was dead. Isn't that hilarious? I don't think I've ever told anyone that."

He pictured her, all stretched out on a plot with her hands folded over her breasts and her eyes closed. In his imagination, she was naked, just as she would be on a prep table.

It was not, as she had posited, hilarious.

He pulled on the edges of his gloves, tightening them.

"You know that place is swimming in arsenic, right?" he said, flatly.

"What?"

"Arsenic. It's what they used before formaldehyde, during the Civil War. And lots of soldiers are buried there."

Hollywood Cemetery, which inspired so much prattling sentimentality, was a damnable network of toxins. The soil's veins were full of poison, snaking their way to the James River. It's why he never drank the tap water. Ever.

"Yeah, this city is totally haunted! Have you ever been to the Poe Museum?"

He had not. He wondered if she believed him about the arsenic, if she cared. He wondered, as she inspected a piece of overcooked broccoli between her bare fingers, if she had washed her hands before coming to the table.

As far as being haunted was concerned, he suspected that if ghosts existed, they existed in Richmond. It was a city that had turned morbidity into industry, and he imagined that even out-of-state ghosts would migrate in for a piece of the action. But in the end, he just couldn't get enthused about the theatrics. The zombie walks and the ghost tours were harmless, bloodless, often eventless encounters.

Besides, nothing in his experience had suggested an afterlife.

"I got this awesome skull-shaped pencil sharpener there. My roommate thinks it's creepy, but she's got this doll collection that is like, way worse."

And there it was. Some remnant of her sad, pedestrian apartment life; a life of thumbtack artwork on eggshell walls; a cramped little box haunted by the cooking smells of a thousand residents, cat litter in the carpet, porcelain dolls on shelves.

Her spine slumped as she shoveled through the remains of her meal, the napkin untouched in her lap, containing only gummy biscuit and nothing more. "So, what about you?" she asked. "Are you going to fess up or what?"

He didn't know what to tell her. His childhood had been embarrassingly normal; he had kept his bike within the perimeter of his subdivision. He hadn't even had any exotic hobbies, nothing obvious that would bond them, and dessert was worryingly imminent.

Frantically, he tried to think of some detail that might set him apart.

"I had a pet squirrel when I was a kid," he said. "His name was Spanky, after the Little Rascal?"

"Oh, come on," she replied, rolling her eyes. "I totally told you an embarrassing secret about myself! I even told you about losing my virginity at an all boy's Catholic school, and you give me Spanky the squirrel?"

He felt guilty, inadequate, flaccid.

"Just tell me something personal. Something sexual maybe?" Her voice dropped on the word *sexual*, and she ran her non-manicured finger around the rim of her water glass.

She was flirting, he supposed. She wanted to hear something illicit, and if he didn't come up with something sexier than Spanky, he would be completely emasculated.

Caught up in the moment maybe, and burdened by the immense pressure to come up with something worthy, he decided to tell her a truth.

"Right about when I turned thirteen," he started, looking deeply into the tablecloth for courage, "I started dipping my fingertips in hot candle wax and then touching things. Just because it felt good, you know? It's like touching something without really touching it... And I liked it so much, that I started doing it all the time, dipping before school, during school, before bed. I used to hide the candles even, like somebody was going to be mad or something if they found out. And I guess..." he stopped. He didn't want to say it; didn't think it was appropriate or even interesting anymore. "And I guess I sort of did it when I masturbated."

Silence.

He held his breath, felt himself going red.

And then, like the sound of war trumpeting over some humiliating hillside, she laughed. She threw her head back, the fillings glinting on her back molars, and she just laughed.

It was mortification, the heat doubling up on him and turning him several unattractive shades of purple. The sound of her became a crashing background hum as he struggled to compose himself.

Why couldn't they have just talked about movies? Why had she made him tell her that?

Then she reached out, and with a hand that may as well have been a claw, she patted him condescendingly on the shoulder.

Patted him.

"Different strokes for different folks," she said, as though that settled everything. "Still... There are some things that are just universally sexy. Like...how about the fact that I'm wearing red lace panties right now?"

That last part, the part about the panties, had been whispered so forcefully that its current carried not just a stench, but a heat.

"Excuse me for a moment," he mumbled, and he sprang from his chair, looking anxiously for that neon sign that said "restroom," that sparkling, safe, oasis in the desert.

He moved like a man obsessed, throwing open the bathroom door and barricading himself stupidly behind it.

Then he went to the sink and ran the water, which he desperately wished to splash on his face, but couldn't. He stared at his reflection in the mirror, and watched the bloated redness work its way back down into his chest and spread sour lava through his extremities. The sink was filthy, he could see that; the gloves absorbed the chill of the porcelain, but reliably kept him out of harms way, just like Dr. Halsted's Caroline Hampton.

He didn't want to go home, to numb another night on the couch, watch a documentary, drink a beer. He was trembling suddenly, from the acid of her touch maybe, or because he was staring down a failure so aggressive that it made him angry.

He was disgusted by her and he despised himself for it, but when he pictured the soft cavities of her genitalia, he imagined the slick of urine there, and the particulate fecal matter hidden in the delicate folds of her anus. It didn't matter what color panties she was wearing, or how painstakingly she managed to bulge her breasts against the table, she was a walking pathogen; a sweating, shitting, shedding receptacle of infection.

Quickly, like a man that senses his monster is just behind him, he put his head down and tunneled his way out of the restaurant.

As he maneuvered through the squash of people, he felt their eyes burrowing into him like hungry, inquisitive larvae, and he wondered how long she would wait before she realized he was gone. Did she already suspect it?

She would be angry or embarrassed, maybe, and wouldn't ever understand why it had become impossible for him to stay. He himself could not immediately see the line that had just been crossed.

The night air hit him with the heady, compost smell of a thousand beetles and worms tilling the soil, every organic thing breathing the stink of respiration and decomposition.

He hated Virginia in July.

The air was pregnant with heat, his lungs clenching with the wet pressure of it. And the crickets and oily toads were singing their nightmare song, the mating song, vibrating every hair in his eardrums.

The sense of failure was oppressive. He was a dud of a date, and no verbal discharging of fun facts and personal confessions would change that.

He didn't realize he was driving down Courthouse Road, or that he was driving at all really, until a stream of Cottonwood trees shook their bony fingers in his periphery.

The air conditioning was finally tuned up, the flow turning glacial, the slick of sweat that covered his skin prickling deliciously. He pictured her, still sitting at the table, waiting on him, her brain already producing the chemicals that would signal her body of the need to defecate. The bacteria in her gut would make up an astounding 60% of her fecal mass when it finally passed.

It wasn't until he saw the sign for Hull Street that he realized he was headed to the mortuary.

On autopilot it had been so natural to gravitate towards work, a place he was at so often, a place where he was respected. And upon thinking about it, he concluded that it was the perfect place to go, considering his mood.

People did not always have the courtesy to die during business hours and, as a consequence, a mortuary was never really closed, never empty. Maybe Sheila or Dave would be there, and maybe they would be happy to see him, happy to have the help. It would stave off the sad inevitability of going home alone.

After the engine was shut off, he had a sense of vultures beating their wings about his skull, and the sound was not unlike that of her laughing, when he had told her about the candle wax.

She would have slept with him, that much was certain. He might have gone with her to her ugly apartment, taken some cheap wine, fucked her under the dead gaze of a hundred doll babies and a couple of cats.

In the dark, he wouldn't have had to look at her. He might have held his breath, used his imagination, suggested doing it in the shower. Instead he had left her wet, ready, and inexplicably undesirable, digesting over an empty plate. He hadn't even given her any money. They would expect her to pay.

A web of guilt fell over him, and as he got out of the car he felt sticky with it, and restricted.

Sheila was there. He could see her in the prep room, bent over a table, her stringy hair pinned back from the greasy plane of her forehead. As he went to her, passing the trays and shelves of familiar chemicals and instruments, she looked up and scrunched her face at him.

"Thought you had a date," she said.

Michael bent over to examine her client, noting the ropey bands of exposed muscle, the crushed shell of the skull, the purple, starburst contusions.

"Car crash," she explained. "Flipped right over on the interstate."

He imagined the big, meaningful flash of the man's last

moment, the terrifying crunch of metal and glass, the car upside down, its wheels still spinning like the kicking legs of an upended June bug. There was a lot of work to be done there.

And he wanted to work; needed to work.

"I'll help you."

"No you won't," she said, pushing slightly into his chest with her clipboard. "It's your only night off this week. You practically live here. Go home."

"Come on Sheila, you can't get this guy by yourself."

"Are you suggesting that I am incapable?" she smiled. She was flirting, Sheila, but in the insincere manner of a waitress or a salesman. "Go home, Michael."

He couldn't tell her that going home was impossible, that the heat of rejection and humiliation was burning him, and before he could compose himself, he was sweating again. He needed cold air. All he could think of, the only thing that made sense to him, was the walk-in storage.

The body-box, they called it.

"I'm just going to check on something," he said. "Then I'll go."

She shook her head, and leaned back towards her client, picking a crust of vomit from his cheek delicately, like she was brushing back the hair on a child's forehead.

The air was so cold that it seemed to hold its own breath.

The body-box was especially full that night, as they had a particularly busy week of funerals ahead. But he knew where he was going. He was going directly to her, to the one he had worked on that morning, and he understood with deepening recognition, that the closer he got to her, the more muted the vultures and the laughter and the failure became.

Stiff and quiet in her plastic bag, she had been drawing him to her.

Margaret Peterson.

Her file had been minimal: came from a good family, worked in dental hygiene, thirty years old, found dead in her bed. There wasn't anything there to tell him who she was.

But when he had looked closely at her, and saw that every stray hair had been plucked, and every blemish had been disguised, he imagined that he knew who she was.

She was a person who had looked closely at herself. Whatever else she had been, she had been aware.

Such was her attention to detail that he hardly had to fix anything at all. She was a miracle of a client, an archetype in skin and hair. Not a lip of fat or a dimple of cellulite anywhere on her. She was someone who had flossed, and worn sunscreen. She was someone who had moisturized.

And within twelve hours she would be positioned in a grey marble casket for the viewing pleasure of her friends and family, and then burned down to a pile of white ash, another beauty lost to the world.

It was sad that Margaret Peterson had so diligently kept after herself, only to end up as an accessory on some vague aunt's mantelpiece.

Slowly, he unzipped the crude plastic case, and thrilled to the sound of the metal teeth opening.

She was pretty. Young. A fallen cake.

Not like his wretched date with her neck creases and cracked cuticles.

He reached out to touch his glove to the brown curl of her hair. Under the preservative, he could smell the vanilla bean shampoo he had used. She was so clean. He had wanted everything to be perfect, just the way she would have wanted it.

And she was perfect; as prepared and beautiful as she would ever be in the world.

And as he sat there, looking at the serenity of her expression, he realized that there was no judgment between them, and no awkward silences over uneaten salad. There was no chance that she was going to suddenly say "totally," or ask him to reveal some horrifying, personal secret.

His breathing had improved. He even laughed at himself then, for the absurdity of his next thought: If only Margaret, no, Maggie, had been his date instead.

The worst ideas begin as insignificant, germinating thoughts. They end with rather hideous habits.

Later, when he thought back to it, he guessed that he did what he did because he was merely curious. Or maybe because that night he had been especially vulnerable. But in the end, the reason was simply not as important as the reward.

The sterile smell of her had been its own rationalization, prompting a need for intimacy in him so powerful that he might as well have been resisting a sniff to a fully bloomed gardenia.

He stopped breathing, just for the duration of taking off his gloves, pulling them slowly so that he could feel the texture of the material as it was sucked from his skin. His fingers were exposed, cold and alien in the oxygen; naked. He slipped them into her right hand, stirred by this violation, her skin touching his, her fingernails just grazing his wrist.

He closed his eyes, taking in a breath to brace against the excruciating sensation of intimacy, her cold hand as immaculate and pure as a saint's.

Just for a moment, a flickering of passion in all of the places in him that had gone dead, and it had begun.

About the Authors

A Look Behind the Stories

Charles Albert studied Theatre at the College of William and Mary, where several of his short plays were produced. After graduating in 2006, he eventually moved Richmond, where he now resides with his wife Gretchen. "Vampire Fiction" is his first published work. The inspiration of which can be accredited to the horrors of everyday life and his personal sarcastic take on the current state of the Horror genre. Charles is inspired by the works of Chuck Palahniuk, Neil Gaiman, and Mike Mignola.

Michael Gray Baughan is writer, researcher, and occasional designer with a degree in English and Creative Writing from the University of Virginia, where he was awarded the Wagenheim Prize for Best Work of Short Fiction. He has authored six books of biography and literary criticism and helped design, composite, or edit numerous others. Baughan lives on the unhip and less haunted Southside of Richmond with his archaeologist wife and increasingly clairvoyant twin daughters. When not writing or parenting, he is usually engaged in other DIY activities like growing food, brewing beer, retrofitting antique radios with digital brains, or stalking the sources of strange noises in the night. "The Rememberist" was born during an uneasy truce between his Yankee birth and his Confederate ancestry.

Beth Brown is the author of several volumes of ghostly history. Her book, *Haunted Plantations of Virginia*, received the 13th

Annual Library of Virginia People's Choice Award for non-fiction, and her most recent title, *Wicked Richmond*, was a nominee for the award the following year. She currently holds the position of senior editor at *Haunted Times Magazine* and serves as a historical and paranormal consultant to a variety of other media outlets. Beth pays homage to Edgar Allan Poe with "Mr. Valdemar" by reinventing his classic and controversial tale "The Facts in the Case of M. Valdemar" for a modern audience.

A Fine Arts graduate of VCU with a face that scared little kids, **Dale Brumfield** is the author of the short story collection *Three Buck Naked Commodes* and three novels: *Remnants: a Novel about God, Insurance and Quality Floorcoverings* and the Kindle- and Nook-compatible eNovels *Trapped Under the Pack-Ice* and *Bad Day at the Amusement Park*. In 1981 he co-founded Richmond's *ThroTTle Magazine* and today is the administrator and sole contributor to that magazine's 30th anniversary website, Throttlemag30.blogspot.com. In addition, Dale is an arts features writer, cartoonist and opinion contributor to Richmond's Style Weekly magazine, and recently won 1st place with the Virginia Press Association and 2nd place nationally with the Association of Alternative Newsweeklies for his investigative cover story on the "lost" 1982 Richmond movie "Rock n' Roll Hotel". Dale lives in Doswell, Virginia with his wife Susan and three teenage children and blogs at Newsfromdoswell.com.

Phil Budahn is a long-time Virginia resident. He credits step-daughter Macon Reed, who graduated from Virginia Commonwealth University in 2007, with introducing him to downtown Richmond and Shockoe Slip. 'Sig's Place' began with the image of an old-fashioned nightclub, the kind of place once called a joint, with silky curtains of cigarette smoke, dark corners that spent decades without the brush of a single sunbeam, and a clientele that made the silence bristle with a sinister allure. Like the fictional Sig, Budahn roamed the city to find the exact spot near the corner of Grace and 5th to place the story and believes if the world didn't have ghosts already, Richmond would have invented them. He also used the city as the setting for a recently completed – and unpublished – trilogy about a unique spectral world and the spirits whose after-lives resemble our own.

Meriah Crawford is an assistant professor at Virginia Commonwealth University, a writer, and a private investigator. Meriah has published several short stories, a range of nonfiction work, and a poem about semicolons, and has a great deal more in the works. As a private investigator for over 8 years, Meriah worked on a wide array of cases including background investigations, insurance accident and theft cases, patent infringement, counterfeiting, harassment, and even a murder. However, she would like to note for the record that she has never killed a client. Yet. Please visit www.mlcrawford.com for more information. The question of figuring out who the good guys are in "Hunting Joey Banks" can be a complicated one as a PI: she thought it would be fun to mix the ethics of a vampire with a whole slew of bad guys and see who would walk away.

James Ebersole was born in Sacramento, California, January 21st, 1990. His family made the coast to coast move to Kure Beach, North Carolina when he was three years old. He didn't do much of the driving to get there. James moved to Richmond, Virginia in 2010, where he currently lives, works at the Poe Museum, and attends the University of Richmond. Previous poems and stories have appeared in such publications as Cape Fear Community College's *Portals* and the University of North Carolina

Wilmington's *Talon Magazine*. The swing set in "The Velveteen Machine" is real. When first working on writing a horror story set in Richmond he just couldn't think of anywhere he'd rather set it than there. James tried to throw in some more distinctly Richmond things in the mix but once he had that one location, everything else in the story just kind of fell into place.

Phil D. Ford is a writer, columnist, musician and radio DJ who has haunted Richmond for a very long time. His work has appeared in *ThroTTle*, *Richmond Magazine* and the Philadelphia-based magazine *Carbon 14*. "231 Creeper" was originally to be a short film; he still wants to make it.

Daniel Gibbs is a 1991 graduate of the College of William and Mary, during which time he began what would be a longstanding love affair with Richmond. He is very proud of having worked at Thalhimers "until the very end," and is particularly interested in the retail and theatrical history of downtown. He hopes to move to Church Hill in the near future -probably right over the Tunnel. An English teacher, he is currently taking time off to write and regain a measure of sanity. Regarding his inspiration for the story: "I had already decided to write one story for each of the City's seven hills, and I thought Pratt's Castle must have been damned freaky, so it just seemed logical that Gamble's Hill would be a story of the bizarre. And, much as I love the city, there's undeniably something creepy about it."

Andrew Goethals has been a cook, teacher, bartender, meat-cutter, house-painter and pet-sitter. He currently divides his time between Richmond and nameless back-country regions, accompanied by a blind dog of incomparable erudition. This is his first appearance in print. His story, "The Conjurer", was inspired by a conversation over brunch about the risks involved in the solitary pursuits of knowledge and perfection.

Eric Hill is the re-incarnation of a Panda who lived peacefully on a Chinese mountainside until it was ravaged by fire in 1135 AD. Not in a hurry to get back to Earth, he popped up in the womb in 1988 surprised because he thought he was going to "Huangnan, China" not "Hampton, Virginia." Eric spends time listening to leaves and sleeping a lot, which is the "panda method". Eric attended Virginia Commonwealth University at an exorbitant rate and believes the American public school system is managed as well as a sex addict manages himself in a brothel. He is studying to become a teacher to fix "this whole [expletive] mess." and currently resides in Roanoke, VA. Eric was inspired to write "The Bike Chain of Fate" because Richmond hipsters are obsessed with their bicycles that it was no great leap to imagine they worshipped them like primitive animists.

Born in Baltimore, **Melissa Scott Sinclair** earned her B.A. in journalism from the University of Delaware. In six years as a reporter for *Style Weekly* in Richmond and *The Virginian-Pilot* in Norfolk, she's written about Confederates, centenarians, mutant catfish and the trial of Beltway sniper Lee Boyd Malvo. She has won 17 awards for her writing from the Virginia Press Association as well as one from the Association of Alternative Newsweeklies. Melissa also worked as a copywriter for Circuit City, where the whispers of cardboard on Layoff Day inspired her story about a corporate ghost.

Native Virginian **Rebecca Snow** grew up within an hour's drive of Richmond. Whether it was her first visit to a Toys R Us or a photo safari with her brother, every trip into town was a treat. She and her husband were married in Hollywood Cemetery on a cloudy day. After the short ceremony, the tiny wedding party ate pizza and an Ellwood Thompson's cake at Bottom's Up. "We're History" was inspired by the fact that she keeps missing the Richmond Zombie Walk. This year, she's bound and determined to shamble with the masses. In addition to preparing for the apocalypse and writing short stories for small presses, she has an online presence at cemeteryflower.blog.com and on Facebook (look for the bloody handprint).

Dawn Terrizzi is a native of Pennsylvania and has lived in Richmond for four years where she has worked within the Henrico County Library System. She is currently earning her Master's degree in Library Science and enjoys reading, writing, painting, playing the drums and traveling. She lives with her wonderful husband, daughter and dogs and hopes to someday raise animals in the country. Dawn has always found trains and train tunnels creepy and thought that a story about the Church Hill Tunnel would be both interesting and spooky.

Amber Timmerman received her Associates degree from Middle Tennessee State University, and is now pursuing an MFA in creative writing. "Maggie," her first published work, was inspired by the delightfully odd history of mortuary science, and was created as a tribute to dysfunctional romances everywhere. She resides in Amelia, Virginia, and is currently working on a new novel and a short story collection.

Acknowledgments

Proper Southern Gratitude

While two people having the same idea around the same time is fairly common, to actually follow through with the idea is another thing completely. We had our first planning meeting at a Thai restaurant in Carytown, discussing which writers we could solicit, where to flyer-bomb "Call for Submissions" leaflets, and most importantly - how soon we wanted to get this project started. The plan was easy, the execution took work, but when those submissions finally came in (and we received a *lot*) we knew it was worth all of our effort just to see how many people had a tale to tell about our River City.

We are now more excited than ever about this book and naturally have several people to thank for this endeavor.

Project –

Thanks to Noah Scalin for his custom artwork and for being as excited as we were about the project; Harry Kollatz, Jr. for the proper Richmond horror introduction; Anne Thomas Soffee for suggesting the editing team; Andrew Blossom for inspiration. Also, we'd like to give a special tip of the hat to all of the city's independent bookstores, musical venues, and other local businesses who have offered to help by hosting events and readings. Your awesomeness is beyond measure.

Personal –

Phil thanks Lisa Kroll for dealing with the manuscripts all over the house; Gina Card, Emily Mandelbaum, and Hope Ford for reading and listening.

Beth thanks Paul and Emma Brown for offering second and third opinions; the staff of Guitar Works for providing a hideout in which to read manuscripts undisturbed.

Special thanks, however, go to anyone whoever winds up in a dark alley, a quiet parking deck, or a haunted bar and daydreams for a fantastic moment that something dark and mysterious might be there.

The Richmond Macabre Team,

Beth Brown
Phil Ford
October 2011

CPSIA information can be obtained at www.ICGtesting.com
Printed in the USA
BVOW010133101011

273132BV00001B/4/P